P9-BAV-033

GHOSTS of WAR
AWOL in North Africa

Other Ghosts of War books

The Secret of Midway

Lost at Khe Sanh

AWOL in North Africa

Fallen in Fredericksburg

GHOSTS of WAR

AWOL in North Africa

STEVE WATKINS

SCHOLASTIC INC.

If you purchased this book without a cover, you should be aware that this book is stolen property. It was reported as "unsold and destroyed" to the publisher, and neither the author nor the publisher has received any payment for this "stripped book."

Copyright © 2016 by Steve Watkins

All rights reserved. Published by Scholastic Inc., *Publishers since 1920*. SCHOLASTIC and associated logos are trademarks and/or registered trademarks of Scholastic Inc.

The publisher does not have any control over and does not assume any responsibility for author or third-party websites or their content.

No part of this publication may be reproduced, stored in a retrieval system, or transmitted in any form or by any means, electronic, mechanical, photocopying, recording, or otherwise, without written permission of the publisher. For information regarding permission, write to Scholastic Inc., Attention: Permissions Department, 557 Broadway, New York, NY 10012.

This book is a work of fiction. Names, characters, places, and incidents are either the product of the author's imagination or are used fictitiously, and any resemblance to actual persons, living or dead, business establishments, events, or locales is entirely coincidental.

ISBN 978-0-545-83706-4

10 9 8 7 6 5 4 3 2 1   16 17 18 19 20

Printed in the U.S.A. 40
First printing 2016
Book design by Yaffa Jaskoll

For Rick and Louie and my dad

My best friend, Greg Troutman, was late for band practice, and our friend Julie Kobayashi wasn't happy about it. I wasn't, either — Greg seemed to be running late a lot lately — but at least I wasn't storming around and yelling about it like Julie. For somebody so quiet at school, she sure could get loud sometimes.

"He better have been abducted by aliens!" she fumed. "Or chased by clowns." She hit a couple of minor chords on her electric keyboard when she said that — *Dunh, dunh DUNNNNH!*

"Why clowns?" I asked.

"Oh, please, Anderson," she said, rolling her eyes — something else she did really well when she was exasperated with Greg or me. "As if there's anything worse. Or scarier."

"He probably had to do chores after school," I suggested.

Julie glared at me. "That's no excuse."

It occurred to me that maybe there *was* something — or somebody — scarier than clowns, but I didn't say that out loud.

Julie stomped around our practice room for another minute, just to make sure I totally got how annoyed she was. We were in the basement of my uncle Dex's junk shop (the Kitchen Sink), of course, where we always practiced, and where, ever since we started our band, the Ghosts of War, we'd been stumbling into ghost mysteries involving this trunk full of old war artifacts. After our most recent ghost episode, I had shoved it deep in a corner of the practice room and piled stuff on top so I wouldn't have to look at it, or be tempted to open it and have another mystery spill out that we'd also have to solve.

We'd already had encounters with two ghosts — one from World War II and the other from the Vietnam War. They turned out to be nice, and we were able to help them in the end, but, man, were we ever stressed out and exhausted afterward. I wrote all about those mysteries in a couple of notebooks I kept hidden under my mattress at home that nobody will ever read except Julie and Greg. I even gave them titles. The first one I called "The Secret of Midway" and the second was "Lost at Khe Sanh."

But all that detective work cut into our band practice time, and the best we'd been able to do in two tries in the monthly open mic night battle of the bands was come in next to last. So I kind of understood why Julie was annoyed right now.

She was still fuming and I was still trying to stay out of her way when the door to our practice room suddenly opened and there was Greg, staggering into the door frame, holding his hand against the side of his head. His red hair was all wild on one side and matted on the other, and when he pulled his hand away from the matted side there was blood. A *lot* of blood!

"Greg!" I shouted, jumping over my amplifier and guitar to get to him before he fainted, or fell, or both.

Julie came flying over to us as well. "Oh my gosh!" she said. "What happened?"

"Uh, maybe we could first stop the bleeding?" Greg said.

I looked around the room but couldn't see anything to use, so I pulled off my shirt.

"What are you doing?" Julie barked. "Put your shirt back on, Anderson."

"Well, what else can I use?" I barked back.

"Go ask your uncle," she said.

Greg shook his head, keeping his hand pressed over the bloody wound. "He must have stepped out. He wasn't at the front desk when I came in."

Then he said, "Check the trunk. I'm pretty sure I saw a medic's kit in there the last time it was open."

"A medic's kit?" I repeated, sort of asking and sort of stalling, so I could think up an excuse not to check. I did *not* want to go back into that trunk and risk starting up another ghost of war mystery.

"Just go check!" Julie ordered. "He's bleeding all over the place. Look, it's on his shirt and everything."

"Okay," I grumbled. "You know, head wounds bleed a lot because the veins or whatever are so close to the skin, but they're usually not that serious. I read that somewhere."

"Go!" Julie ordered again.

It took me a couple of minutes to drag boxes and stuff off the trunk, but once again — just like the last two times this happened — the trunk seemed to practically open by itself. And sure enough, there, right on top, was a canvas army medic's pouch. I hesitated, then grabbed it and opened it and rifled through scissors and vials and capped syringes and pill bottles and stuff until I found what seemed to be gauze packages, and a larger package that said "tourniquet." I grabbed both and rushed back over to Julie and Greg, tearing open the packages as I went.

"Smells kind of musty," Julie said as I handed her the gauze. She wrinkled her nose but pressed it against Greg's wound. I offered her the tourniquet, too, but she just shoved it away.

"We don't need that, Anderson. We need some tape, to tape this on."

So I went back for the medical kit — there were rolls of surgical tape — and we finished bandaging Greg.

"Should we call 911?" I asked.

"I guess," Julie said, though she didn't sound convinced.

"What?" I asked. "You don't think we should?"

"Well, we should see how serious it is first," she said. "And you know what happened the last time we called 911."

Of course I did — we all did. It was when I found a hand grenade in the trunk a month earlier, which I wrote all about in "Lost at Khe Sanh." The bomb squad had to detonate it. Uncle Dex said we couldn't keep practicing at the Kitchen Sink if we ever did anything like that again.

Greg spoke up. "Don't call 911. I'm okay. I think."

He sat up straighter.

"Are you sure?" I asked, feeling guilty that we were even debating this. Of *course* we should call 911.

"Yes," he said. "I'm sure."

"Maybe we should call your dad, then?" I suggested.

"No, it's okay," Greg replied. "I just got a little freaked out."

"Well, who wouldn't?" Julie said, sounding so sympathetic it was almost hard to remember how annoyed she had been earlier at the missing Greg.

"All that blood," I added.

"So what happened anyway?" Julie asked. "Did you wreck your bike?"

"Yeah, was it a bike wreck?" I echoed Julie. "Or did you have a run-in with a clown?"

Julie gave me a very dirty look.

"Neither one," Greg said, taking it all in stride, as if a guy with a bloody head got asked every day if he'd gotten in a clown fight.

"Well, what, then?" Julie asked — or demanded.

Greg got a goofy expression on his face, and I could tell he was embarrassed.

"It was a chicken," he admitted.

"A chicken?" I repeated. "What about a chicken?"

"It flew into my head."

"A chicken?" I said again. "Flew into your head?"

Greg nodded. Julie frowned. "Chickens don't fly," she said.

I was happy to correct her. "Actually, they do, Julie. Short distances. That's just a myth that they can't fly at all."

She gave me the stink eye and I stopped smiling.

"Well, it didn't exactly fly on its own," Greg said. "And it wasn't exactly the kind of chicken you guys are thinking it was."

"What kind was it, then?" Julie demanded.

Greg grinned, but then he winced. I guess grinning hurt his head. He held something up I hadn't realized he had been holding all this time in his non-bloody hand. It was a rubber chicken.

"Are you serious?" Julie asked.

"Pretty crazy, huh?" Greg said. "I was just minding my own business, riding my bike over here past that old Masonic cemetery, when I saw something out of the corner of my eye, flying right at me, but before I could duck, it hit me and I crashed my bike."

"So somebody threw it at you?" I said. "Somebody in the cemetery."

"A ghost," Julie said.

Greg and I looked at her to see if she was kidding. It wasn't like we needed any convincing that ghosts were real. But why would someone throw a rubber chicken at Greg — or at anybody?

Julie laughed. "Oh my gosh, you two are so gullible! I was just kidding."

"Not funny," I said. "Under the circumstances."

Greg shrugged. "I thought it was kind of funny," he said. "In an understated sort of way." That was an expression he'd picked up from Julie, who used a lot of adult expressions that most kids didn't quite understand, especially kids in middle school like us.

"Do you remember anything else?" I asked.

"Not really," Greg said. "Just, you know, picking up the rubber chicken, and my bike, and then coming over here. A couple of people saw me and must have seen all the blood because they got these funny looks on their faces. One guy asked if I needed any help. I just waved the chicken and said I was okay. Guess I was a little woozier than I realized."

He paused, before adding, "Oh wait. There was this loud pop sound just before the chicken hit me. That was over in the cemetery, too."

"What do you think it was?" Julie asked.

Greg didn't get a chance to answer, though, because a voice behind us, from the direction of the trunk in the corner of the practice room, interrupted.

"There's sulfa powder in my kit," it said. "You should pour some over the boy's wound, make sure it doesn't get infected until we can get him off the battlefield. And keep pressure on the wound."

We all turned and stared. It was obviously another ghost — and obviously a soldier — but no matter how many times these ghosts showed up, it was impossible not to be shocked.

The new ghost was wearing tattered green army fatigues, his face mostly blackened from what looked like dirt and smoke. He had a Red Cross armband on — red cross with a white square — and he was looking around the room as if expecting to see, well, I didn't know what. Just something else. Or somewhere else.

"No stretcher?" the man asked.

I shook my head and said, "No, sir."

"All right, then," the man said. "I guess we'll just have to stitch him up right here."

He had somehow crossed the room without my realizing it, and was reaching for the medical kit. Only his hand stopped short when he tried to pick it up, as if it was too heavy, or as if he couldn't quite get a grip on it, or as if it was solid and he wasn't.

"This is strange," he said, shaking his head.

And then he vanished.

CHAPTER 2

"Wait!" I yelled, jumping to my feet, holding out the pouch, as if he might want to take it. "Come back!"

Greg was standing next to me. "Wasn't he supposed to, you know, fade out? That's what the other ghosts did. They didn't just suddenly disappear like that."

"Well, they're all different, aren't they?" said Julie. "Just like people. And ghosts are people, too."

"Uh, not exactly," I said.

"Of course they are," Greg said, probably agreeing with Julie because it was easier than disagreeing with Julie, who had to be right about everything — and usually was.

"Well, whatever," I said. "But shouldn't we be focusing on bloody Greg here?"

Bloody Greg lifted the gauze from his forehead. The bleeding seemed to have stopped.

We didn't have a chance to inspect further just then because we heard footsteps coming down the stairs from the store above us.

This time it was Uncle Dex.

"What in the world is going on?" he demanded. "There's a bike lying on the sidewalk at the front door, and blood on the front doorknob!"

Greg waved the gauze. "Sorry," he said. "That was me. I got hit by a rubber chicken."

"Whoa!" Uncle Dex said, pulling off his baseball cap and kneeling. "You okay? Let me take a look."

He quickly determined that the bleeding had, in fact, stopped, then he went upstairs for his own first aid kit, which took him a while to find. He had more gauze, though, and alcohol for cleaning the wound, and when he came back down, he went to work on Greg, and in a minute had him all cleaned off and a bandage taped to Greg's forehead.

"Flesh wound," he announced. "Not going to need stitches."

"That's not what the ghost said," I muttered to Julie.

"What's that?" Uncle Dex asked.

"Um, nothing," I said. "Just, you know, thanks for coming to the rescue."

Uncle Dex laughed. "Nothing much to rescue. Just a cleanup operation. Not sure I can do anything about this shirt, though."

Greg shrugged. "That's okay."

"Good," Uncle Dex said. "Now tell me about this rubber chicken that attacked you. Could you identify him in a police lineup?"

Greg held up the bird. "No need for that. Got him right here." He told Uncle Dex what he'd already told Julie and me — about the Masonic cemetery, and the pop, and getting hit, and the rest.

"Hmm," Uncle Dex said. "Sounds like a sneak attack. You kids have any enemies who would pull a prank like that?"

We all looked at one another. Did we have any enemies? Of *course* we had enemies. This eighth grader named Belman, and his friends, who were always trying to bully us at school, and who had a band, too, and always won the all-ages open mic competitions, while we just mostly stunk.

"Not really," Julie said, responding to Uncle Dex's question about our enemies. I could tell by the look on Julie's face that if Belman *was* responsible for the rubber chicken attack, she was determined we would take care of him ourselves.

"Okay," Uncle Dex said. "Well, probably just a random thing, then. I'll make some calls when I go back upstairs, just to be on the safe side. See if my friend down at the police station has heard about anybody else getting pelted by rubber chickens or anything strange like that."

We all thanked him, and then he left, and finally we were able to exhale and stutter and stammer about what all had just happened. It was too much, really: rubber chicken attacks, and new ghosts with medical kits, and appearances and disappearances so sudden that we all practically had whiplash.

"Do you think he'll come back?" Greg asked. He was talking about the ghost, not Uncle Dex.

"Yeah," I said. "Probably. The other ones came to my

house first. You remember. Just showed up in my room. So maybe it will be the same with this one. Even though he came here first, and saw all of us and not just me."

"They *are* all different," Julie reminded us. "Like I said before."

"I guess so," I said. "But, meanwhile, why don't we look over this medical kit to see if there are any clues? If he's like the other ghosts, he's not going to know who he is, or where he's from, or what happened to him."

"Yeah," Greg said. "Another missing in action."

"Perhaps we should show your uncle the medical kit," Julie suggested. "Since he knows so much about antiques, and about old military items. He might be able to tell us what war it's from, anyway. And what branch of the service. Also, I'm not sure we should go rummaging around inside there by ourselves, because we have no idea what might be in there."

"You mean like another hand grenade?" Greg asked eagerly.

"She means like those hypodermic needles we already saw," I said. "And whatever's in those medicine bottles. And whatever that is the ghost mentioned — the sulfur."

"He said sulfa, not sulfur," Greg said. "I'm pretty sure."

"Maybe they're the same thing," I responded. "Maybe he has some kind of accent. You know, drops his *r*'s."

"Let's just go ask your uncle about it," Julie said again, and this time we all agreed.

.   .   .

"World War II vintage, definitely," Uncle Dex said as soon as we handed him the kit upstairs. "And army." He carefully pulled all the items out and laid them in a row on the counter naming them as he went: adhesive plaster, iodine swabs, blunt forceps, Mercurochrome, ammonia inhalants, adhesive compresses, aspirin, safety pin cards, burn ointment, a thermometer, those sulfa packets the ghost mentioned. There were also things called litter straps, and an Emergency Medical Tag book with strings attached to detachable tags and places to record identification, branch of service, diagnosis, and treatment. Uncle Dex told us what most of this stuff was, and he said the strings were to tie the medical tags to the buttons on wounded soldiers' uniforms on the battlefield.

As usual, there weren't any other customers in the Kitchen Sink. Late Tuesday afternoon in downtown Fredericksburg, Virginia, isn't exactly the liveliest place on the planet, and even less so in the dozen junk shops — I mean, antique stores — on Caroline and Sophia Streets, including my uncle's.

"You have most everything you'd need here if you were an army medic," Uncle Dex concluded.

I thought he was finished, but he paused for a second, tapped his chin, and asked us, "Notice anything missing?"

He studied our faces in anticipation of our guesses, since obviously we wouldn't have a clue.

Boy, was I wrong.

"Penicillin," Julie said. "To fight infections. I wrote a research paper on penicillin in fourth grade. I got an A."

If any other sixth grader had said this, Greg and I would have been really shocked. But Julie was so smart that it didn't surprise us anymore when she knew really random things.

"Right," Uncle Dex said. "They weren't able to mass produce penicillin until near the end of the war. That's why early on they had to use sulfa instead. It helped fight infections some, and was the best they had at the time. They'd sprinkle or sometimes just dump it onto wounds when they were trying to save guys who'd been shot."

He hesitated for a second and then asked, "Notice anything else missing?"

Even Julie was stumped this time, so Uncle Dex answered his own question. "Quinine. Because the Japanese had it all, and nobody else — the Allies, anyway — could get any. That was why early in the war, malaria was such a big problem for our soldiers — the ones fighting in the Pacific and North Africa. Malaria is a disease you can get from mosquitos that causes really high, dangerous fevers."

He waited for us to ask him some more questions about the whole quinine thing, but nobody did, so he just continued on his own. "They make quinine from the bark of special trees that mostly just grow in the Philippines and other places the Japanese captured early in the war in the Pacific. So that's why there's none here in this medic's bag, and why there was none for the Allies, until they came up with a man-made replacement later in the war."

"Anything else you can tell us about the medical kit?" Greg asked, ready to move on to information we maybe could actually use, not that the history of quinine wasn't interesting and all.

"Well," Uncle Dex said, turning the canvas bag over in his hands, inspecting the straps, and the various scissors and other pill bottles and stuff. "I'd say it belonged to a private, or a noncommissioned officer in the medical corps."

"How come?" I asked.

"No surgical equipment," he said. "Just first aid items, things you'd need behind the lines to treat infections and headaches and muscle sprains, and most important, stuff for stabilizing battlefield wounds and injuries, keeping soldiers alive so litter bearers could get them back to safety off the battlefield, and ambulances could get them back to surgical units in the rear. Surgeons were officers. Medics were enlisted men."

"Uh, 'litter bearers'?" Greg asked. "Nothing to do with picking up trash, right?"

"A litter was what they called a stretcher back then," I said. "For carrying wounded guys, like Uncle Dex said."

"Oh, right. Got it," Greg replied. "Well, anyway, wouldn't it be cool to, um, know who the medic's kit *actually* belonged to? Like the actual person? You know, so we could return it to him, or to his family?"

"Oh, that shouldn't be too hard," Uncle Dex said.

All three of us stared at him.

"Really?" Julie said. "You can help us find out?"

"That would be awesome!" Greg said.

"Yeah!" I added. "But how? It's just a medical kit. Even if we know it's from World War II and belonged to somebody who wasn't an officer, how can you figure out anything else just from what's there?"

Uncle Dex laughed. "Easy, like I said." He reached inside the bag and fished for something on the bottom.

"His identification card is right here."

CHAPTER 3

On the cover it said "United
States of America War Department," and under that was
"Medical Department" and "Red Cross" and "Identification
Card." An ID number was stamped at the bottom. Inside
was a black-and-white picture of the man we'd seen earlier —
or, rather, a younger, cleaner, happier version of the man.
And his race and birth date and eye color and height:
Caucasian. March 6, 1923. Brown. 5'10". There was also a
military authorization signature, along with a date and place:
Philadelphia, Pennsylvania. And a rank: corporal.

And, of course, a name.

"John Wollman." Greg said it out loud.

"*Corporal* John Wollman," Julie corrected him.

I just said, "Wow." And I was pretty sure I was thinking what Greg and Julie were thinking, too: that this was going to be the easiest ghost of war mystery we'd had to solve so far. In the past we'd knocked ourselves out just trying to figure out the names of the ghosts. Now, though, we were practically done!

"Does it give the name of whatever army unit he was in?" I asked.

"It doesn't look like it," Uncle Dex said. "So he was probably either assigned to a medical corps battalion that ran medical facilities near the front lines, or a field hospital away from the battle. Or he could have been assigned to an infantry squad or platoon, going with them into battle to try to save lives and help the wounded there. They might rotate a medic from one to the other, I suppose."

He gave us a minute to absorb all that, then Uncle Dex said, "So there you go. All you have to do is track down John Wollman's family — and I'm betting you could start by aiming your search at Philadelphia, since it looks like maybe that was where he signed up for the army — and you can send them his medic's pouch. And I won't even charge you anything for it."

He winked at me. "You kids *did* find it in my basement, right?"

"Thanks, Uncle Dex," I said. I started to scoop all the contents back into John Wollman's medic pouch, but Uncle Dex stopped me.

"Not so fast," he said. "I should probably confiscate these first." He picked up the syringes and the morphine vials and dropped them in a box behind the counter. "Pretty sure none of your parents would want you going around carrying narcotics."

Greg didn't get it. "What narcotics?"

Julie explained this one, too. "Morphine is a painkiller and it's not supposed to be used anywhere except in hospitals. During the war, they gave it to soldiers who had been wounded and were in a lot of pain on the battlefield."

"Got it," Greg said as I packed the rest of the stuff back into the medical kit. And then the three of us headed back to the basement to sort everything out. Not the stuff in the kit, but the crazy events of the afternoon.

I half expected to see the ghost down there waiting for us, and I looked forward to telling him his name, and showing him all the information on his identification card, and having him remember everything that had happened to him.

We had such great information to prompt his memory, I figured it might even be enough to help him remember his entire story — how he died and disappeared and everything — and maybe even go off today to wherever the ghosts go once they have their answers to how they came to be missing in action, and once they've found their peace.

Greg and I sat on our amplifiers. Julie plopped down at her electric keyboard. We stared at one another for a minute, with the occasional glance over to the corner of the practice room and the trunk, which somebody had closed, though I didn't remember doing that earlier.

I fiddled with the canvas medical bag, tracing the outline of the Red Cross symbol.

"So what now?" Greg asked, breaking the silence.

"We get to work," Julie said. "Trying to find out more about him. Doing our research."

"I don't know," Greg said. "Maybe we should wait and see if he just, you know, remembers stuff for himself."

"Julie's right," I said, "but it's late already, and we don't even have any practice time left today, so why don't we get going on research at home and we can text one another about it later."

"Okay. Besides, I have to go to a meeting," Greg said. He didn't say what kind of meeting and Julie and I didn't ask because we already knew. Since his dad stopped drinking a month ago, Greg had been going to Al-Anon meetings, for family members of people with drinking problems. He didn't like to talk about it, though he sometimes said things to me when we were alone, like one night when just out of the blue he said, "I might think I've had a hard time with my dad, but there are people at these meetings that have had it a lot worse."

And then we moved on to other things.

"All right," Julie said with a sigh. "But just because this looks like it will be easy — because we already know our ghost's name — I just have a feeling that it's going to be more complicated this time. A *lot* more."

· · ·

After that, we trudged upstairs and went our separate ways, all of us dazed. I barely remembered to say good-bye and thanks to Uncle Dex, or much of anything else until I was two blocks away and realized I was right next to the stone wall around the Masonic cemetery. I nervously stopped and got off my bike and went over to the wall. The stones were slick, and it took a minute to find a place to climb up so I could peer over the top. I could have gone around the block to the iron gate, but sometimes that was locked.

The cemetery was empty — except for the people buried there, of course. Not that I expected to see whoever threw or launched the rubber chicken at Greg. They must have been long gone by then. But still, you just never know with these mysteries and how you'll end up figuring them out, whether it's about a rubber chicken or a new ghost.

It was good that I stopped, because I found Greg's beanie in the grass next to the wall. He wore it all the time. The rubber chicken must have knocked it off. I stuck it in my backpack to give to him the next day, but texted him that I had it so he wouldn't worry.

Mom and Dad were just sitting down to eat when I walked in.

"Hurry and wash your hands," Mom called out. "We're having lasagna."

Lasagna for dinner meant one of two things. Either Mom was feeling better from her MS — multiple sclerosis — and had been in the kitchen cooking, or else she hadn't made dinner and Dad had picked up takeout on his way home from work.

It turned out to be the first one: Mom *was* feeling better. MS is an autoimmune disease that sometimes makes her really weak, and can get so bad it's almost like she's paralyzed in her arms and legs. The MS never goes away, and generally gets worse as you get older, but it can also be a little easier to live with at certain times. Like tonight. I even heard Mom singing when I came out of the bathroom. Dad was singing, too. Some old Beatles song. They both liked the Beatles. I did, too, come to think of it. This one was called "Got to Get You into My Life," and next thing I knew I was humming along with them, and thinking maybe our band could do a Beatles song.

"Hey, buddy," Dad said. "Good day?"

I nodded. "We didn't get to practice much, though. Greg got hit by a rubber chicken."

Mom burst out laughing but somehow managed to stop herself and said we should say the blessing first, and then I could tell them all about it. Halfway through saying grace, Dad snorted and started laughing, too. Mom had to say the "Amen!"

It turned out to be about the nicest dinner we'd had in a while. I told them all about Greg and his bloody head and the rubber chicken and the medic's pouch, leaving out the part about the medic himself showing up. They were kind of concerned, but mostly kept laughing because it all seemed pretty ridiculous, plus I told the story pretty well. I always liked it when Mom and Dad thought I was funny and we all could sit around and just talk about stuff, the way we used to before Mom got sick. We even had ice cream for dessert, which we almost never did at our house. I had mine with chocolate syrup.

•　•　•

The ghost showed up later, just as I expected, and just as I was getting ready for bed. I nearly ran into him when I came back from brushing my teeth.

We both did a double take.

"Whoa! Sorry to startle you," he said.

"That's okay," I squeaked, skirting around him and inching over to my bed. I wasn't scared exactly. But I couldn't help being nervous.

He sat in the chair next to my desk and computer. "Your friend doing all right?" he asked. "He get treatment?"

"Oh, well, it wasn't that bad of a cut," I said. "It stopped bleeding. He didn't need stitches after all."

The ghost — John Wollman — *Corporal* Wollman — nodded. "Good to hear. Hate to see a man down."

I waited in case he was going to say anything else, but when he didn't I decided to get the conversation going again myself. "I guess you're here because you need us to help you, right?"

Corporal Wollman blinked. "I do?"

"Well, yes," I said. "I mean, that's usually how it works. That's how it worked the other two times."

He blinked again. "The other two times of what?"

"Of ghosts," I said. "Who showed up here, like you did."

He seemed confused. "I guess I'm a little lost or something," he said. "Afraid I don't quite know what you're saying there."

I sat up cross-legged on my bed. "You do know you're a ghost, don't you?" I asked.

He lifted his arm and stared at his hand, then lifted his other arm and stared at his other hand. Both were the same — solid but not quite.

"Huh," he said. And that's all. Just "huh," as if it hadn't occurred to him before that he was a ghost, or as if he'd just woken up from a really, really, really long sleep, like Rip Van Winkle.

Then he said, "Maybe you could, uh, explain some more about what's going on here. I'm not sure what to make of this ghost business. Or how my hands look. Or what's been happening. The last I knew I was in North Africa."

"North Africa?" I said. "What were you doing there?"

He rubbed his chin for a second, shook his head as if clearing away cobwebs, and said, "Funny, but I can't seem to quite remember that, either. Except there was the war with the Germans. And that's where they sent us. And —"

He stopped. Rubbed harder. Then said, "And I guess I do need your help after all."

CHAPTER 4

And then he disappeared again —
just as suddenly as before at the Kitchen Sink.

Julie was right: these ghosts were all different from one
another, not only in how they looked and talked and how old
they were and where they came from, but also in how and
when and where they showed up, and how long they stayed,
and how quickly they vanished. None of it made a whole lot
of sense, but I guess that's just the way it is when you're dead,
but not quite done with the life you left behind.

I called Greg right away and didn't even wait for him
to say anything before I launched into the story about what
had just happened — about John Wollman showing up

suddenly, and not seeming to realize that he was a ghost, and saying something about North Africa, and the war, and then just suddenly being gone.

"And what the heck is this about a war in Africa?" I said. "Why would they send the army to Africa? I thought we fought the Germans in, like, France and Germany. Somewhere in Europe, anyway."

Greg still hadn't said anything, so I figured I should give him a chance to speak. "Well?" I asked. "What do you make of all this?"

Greg didn't answer. His dad did.

"Anderson?" he said. "That's a pretty wild story you've got there. Is this something you boys are writing for school? Greg didn't mention an assignment."

I froze. Oh no! What was I supposed to do now?

"Anderson?" Greg's dad said again. "You still there?"

"Yes, sir," I said. "Uh, so is Greg there? I, um, need to talk to him about, uh, yeah, about the story we're writing. Together. It's a group project. You know, to make up a story and everything. For history class. About the war. So, uh, this was the idea we came up with. A ghost from World War II."

"I see," Mr. Troutman said. "Well, Greg's in the shower. He left his phone out here in the living room."

"Okay," I said. "Would you ask him to call me when he gets out?"

Mr. Troutman said he would and then we both hung up and I couldn't believe what an idiot I'd just been and how close I'd come to spilling the secret about the ghosts of war. I still couldn't say why it was so important not to let grown-ups know about this stuff. I just knew it was. At the very least they would think Greg and Julie and I were crazy, and they might not let us hang out together anymore or be in our band.

Or they might just stick us in a mental hospital, because that's probably what I would do if I found out my kid was convinced he had been talking to ghosts.

It was nearly an hour before Greg called me back. "Oh man!" he said. "You told my dad!"

"It was an accident," I said. "He answered your phone. And, anyway, he just thinks we're writing a story for school."

"I know, I know," Greg said. "But still. I just about had a heart attack when he told me what you said."

"But he thinks we're making this up, right?"

"Yes," Greg said. "He started asking me a bunch of questions, and when he realized I knew zero about it, he went off on this giant history lesson explaining to me about the war in North Africa."

"What did he say?" I asked.

"A ton of stuff," Greg said. "He even made me take notes, since he thinks it's for a school project. And thanks a lot, by the way. I had to make up all kinds of things to explain that. I hate lying to my dad."

"Sorry."

"Yeah. Well, I guess we sort of have to. Anyway, he said that's where the war started — for the Americans, I mean. Against the Germans and the Italians. That part of the war."

We had already learned plenty about the war against the Japanese — or at least the early part of the war, and this hugely important navy battle called the Battle of Midway, which the U.S. won, and which, if we'd lost, would have probably meant we'd lose the war against the Japanese for control of the Pacific. And maybe all of World War II. That research had been kind of awkward at times because Julie's mom is Caucasian and was born in America while her dad is Japanese, but the Japanese connection ended up being a big help to us in the end.

So we definitely knew plenty about the war in the Pacific. What we didn't know a lot about — or enough about, anyway — was the war in Europe.

"The Germans took over Austria in 1938 and invaded Poland in 1939, you do know that, right?" Greg asked. "Those are countries right next to Germany."

"Yeah, that part I know. We learned it in history class last year. Is this in your notes from your dad?" I asked.

"Yes. That's where he started from," he said. "Okay, so then the Germans picked off just about all the other countries in Europe, one by one, including Belgium and Denmark and the Netherlands and Greece and France and you name it. Except Italy and Spain. They were both fascist countries, and Italy even became a German ally in 1940. You know about fascism, right?"

"A little bit," I said. "It's the name for the type of government. And it meant they also had dictators like Adolf Hitler, and nobody was allowed to question anything. They would arrest or, like, assassinate anybody who went against them."

"Right," Greg said. "And they believed that their countries were superior to everybody else's. Germany was the absolute worst. Hitler said the German people were, like, this master race, and because of that they had a right to take over any country they wanted, and if they needed their oil or natural resources or anything, they just took it. And if there was anybody they thought was lesser than them, they might make them work as basically just slaves, or they might kill them, in death camps, like they did to the Jewish people. Millions of people . . ." His voice trailed off.

I shook my head and said, "That's terrible," but that didn't seem nearly strong enough. No words I could think of were.

"I know," Greg said. "My dad got so worked up talking about Hitler and the Nazis. But the crazy thing is that for two years the U.S. just sat on the sidelines and didn't send our army to help, not even in England when the Nazis were bombing them for, like, months and months. Out of all those countries in Europe, England was the only one that refused to surrender, and Hitler couldn't defeat them without his ground troops and his tanks, which he couldn't get across the English Channel."

"So we just sat there and didn't do anything?" I said, incredulous.

"My dad said it was complicated," Greg said. "Because the American people didn't want another war. World War I was supposed to have been the war to end all wars, and that was obviously turning out to be a big lie. But we did do some things to help. Some important things, like sending guns and tanks and bombs and anything we could to help England."

"And then in 1941 the Japanese attacked us," I said. "Which basically meant we *had* to go to war. So we declared war on Japan. And then Germany declared war on us because Japan was their ally. Which meant that we had to declare war on Germany."

"Right," Greg said. "And since Germany declared war on the U.S., Italy did, too."

Just thinking about everyone declaring war on everyone else made my head spin. Like Greg's dad said, complicated.

Greg kept talking. "Did you know that the French also made a deal with the Germans — my dad called it a deal with the devil — that if Germany didn't move their army into all of France, just, like, stayed mostly in Paris and on the French coast to guard the English Channel, that France would cooperate with them and wouldn't fight them? France got to still mostly govern themselves and their colonies in North Africa. As long as they did what the Germans told them to do. They called it the Vichy government, because that was the town where the French had to relocate their capital after the Germans conquered Paris."

"And those colonies in Africa? What was that all about?" I was really impressed by how much Greg had learned from his dad already since I'd called. Maybe our brains grow as we get older, and maybe Greg's brain was going through a growth spurt. Or maybe he'd just managed to take really good notes.

"I didn't know anything about the colonies in Africa," Greg said. "I mean, I didn't even know anyone had colonies in Africa. But it turns out that most of the countries in Europe conquered the different countries in Africa and Asia back in, like, the 1800s. They set up their own governments there."

"Sort of like when the British came to America," I said.

"Yeah. So the French were in control over most of the countries in North Africa — the ones on the Mediterranean Sea. Morocco, Algeria, and Tunisia. And the Vichy government was in charge of those at the start of World War II. Putting them on the side of Germany and Italy."

I was pretty sure there were other countries in North Africa on the Mediterranean, but I wasn't too great at geography and couldn't name them right off the top of my head.

But Greg knew. "Well, there's Libya," he said. "That's

next to Tunisia, to the east, and it was under Italian rule. Next to that was Egypt, which didn't belong to anyone, exactly, but the British did have an army there and kind of oversaw things."

Thinking about how upset American colonists were under British rule, I said, "That wasn't very nice to the people who already lived there," I said. "All those Tunisians and Libyans and Egyptians."

"Yeah," Greg said. "I don't think people thought much about that back then, though — whether it was right or wrong to have colonies in Africa or wherever. Kind of like how European settlers didn't think too much about the Native Americans when they came over to America and took all their land and everything."

We both thought about that for a minute, before going back to the conversation about why the U.S. war against Germany started in North Africa.

"Well, here's what my dad told me," Greg said. "President Franklin Roosevelt and the U.S. generals decided they couldn't just invade Europe straight on to fight Nazi Germany because that meant crossing the English Channel and attacking the Germans in France. The French coast was too heavily fortified by the Germans, making it easy for them to take out our ships, especially with their submarines. The Allies figured they needed to get control of the Mediterranean Sea and the North Atlantic. If they controlled those, then they could send supplies and weapons and men over without German interference. So the Americans decided to conquer North Africa first to get control of the Mediterranean. Then they could fight their way up through Italy and defeat the Italians. And then, with the Italians out of the way, they could attack the Germans from the south and at the same time from the west, across the English Channel. My dad called it the underbelly of Europe, or something like that."

"So that's what the war in North Africa was all about!" I said. "Sort of a second staging area with England, for attacking the Germans and the Italians in Europe. Who knew?"

"Apparently a lot of people knew," Greg said. "Like my dad. And maybe everybody but us."

"The ghost knew," I said. "But that was about all he could remember."

"Did you at least tell him his name?" Greg asked.

"Not yet," I said. "He disappeared too fast, just like he did before. It made me so dizzy I fell off the bed."

"Really?" Greg said. "Wow."

"Not really," I added. "But it *was* fast — the way he disappeared."

"Guess we better be ready, then," Greg said. "For when he *re*appears, in case it's that fast again, too."

CHAPTER 5

There was more history, of course. There's always more history. But there was also remembering we had to get up for school in the morning, plus Greg ran out of notes because his dad hadn't gotten to finish the story about how the U.S. went to war in North Africa.

So Greg and I got off the phone. He was yawning so much that I could hardly understand what he was saying anyway. I was so tired I was sure I'd fall asleep as soon as my head touched my pillow, but instead I lay awake for what felt like half the night, my head spinning over everything that had happened that day. A new ghost suddenly shows up in your life and you don't exactly get used to that sort of thing, even if it has happened to you twice before.

John Wollman. Army medic. Corporal. Philadelphia. The war in North Africa. Hitler. Tunisia. Egypt. A deal with the devil. Death camps. Vichy France. Rubber chickens.

It all swam together — all those things we'd been talking about, and that I knew I was going to have to learn a lot more about if we were going to help the new ghost. I wondered if he would come back tonight, and since I couldn't fall asleep, I hoped so — at least I could tell him his name.

He didn't, though. And I finally fell asleep anyway.

•　　•　　•

We filled Julie in on everything the next day at lunch — me about my brief visit with John Wollman, Greg about everything else. I could tell Julie was impressed by all Greg knew, the same as I had been.

She even said, "Very impressive" when he finished, which was a high compliment coming from Julie, who always wanted to be the most impressive person around.

Greg grinned a very big grin. "Thanks," he said.

"Meanwhile, you'll never guess what I found out in a World War II causalities database," Julie said. She didn't wait for us to answer. "A medical corps corporal named John

Wollman is listed as AWOL — Absent Without Official Leave. He disappeared in Tunisia in April 1943."

She was about to say more when a shadow darkened our table. We all looked up, though we knew who it was even before we confirmed it.

"Hello, Belman," Julie growled.

Belman, who was in eighth grade and our self-appointed archenemy, helped himself to my carton of chocolate milk, or tried to.

"Hey," Greg said, grabbing it back. "Knock it off. This is a no-bullying zone. The whole school is."

Belman grinned his own big grin. "So sorry, midgets. You're all so tiny, I didn't even notice you there. I thought somebody had just left a carton of milk here all for me."

His friends — Julie had started calling them the Three Stooges since we didn't know their actual names — all laughed as if anything Belman said was actually funny. Which it wasn't. Usually.

Then they all started clucking like chickens for some reason, and laughing even harder. We tried to ignore them, though it was pretty much impossible.

Belman and the Three Stooges finally finished clucking after about a minute, which seemed like forever, then he patted each one of us on the head like we were little kids, and strutted off across the cafeteria to harass some other sixth graders, with the Stooges trailing behind him.

I felt humiliated, the way I usually did when stuff like that happened and I couldn't do anything about it. Julie grinded her teeth.

Greg just sat there and fumed.

"What was with all the clucking?" I said to try and get us out of this low place.

"Who knows?" said Greg.

Julie sat up straight all of a sudden and actually said, "Aha!"

"Aha what?" I asked.

"Yeah," Greg said, rousing himself a little. "Aha what?"

Julie got a really serious look on her face. "Aha I know why they did that. It was because they must have been the ones who hit Greg with the rubber chicken."

Greg and I stared at each other, then we both started nodding.

"Makes sense, I guess," Greg said. "I mean, why else would they do that?"

"But we still don't have any proof," I said.

Julie made a fist and quietly pounded the table. "Then we'll just have to go get some."

I had no idea how we were going to do that, but then I figured if we were able to solve ghost mysteries, we ought to be able to get the goods on Belman and the rubber chicken attack, too.

"Meanwhile," said Julie, "just so you know, you two weren't the only ones doing ghost research last night. In addition to finding out that John Wollman was AWOL in the war in North Africa, I may have found somebody who would know about him."

"No way!" I exclaimed. "How? Who? Where?"

Julie smiled. "The Internet. John Wollman III. And Philadelphia, just like your uncle Dex said."

I couldn't believe Julie had waited this long to tell us her news.

She shrugged. "Greg was so excited about everything, I didn't want to interrupt. And then Belman showed up."

"That was very nice of you," Greg said, sounding almost formal about it. "Thanks."

"You're welcome," Julie said.

If I didn't know better, I would have almost thought they were, like, flirting or something. As soon as the thought came to me I smacked myself in the forehead to make it go away.

"What did you do that for?" Greg asked, looking at me oddly.

"Just remembered something," I said.

"What?" Julie asked.

I was stumped. Usually I could make stuff up pretty quickly, but this time my mind was a blank. "I guess I already forgot."

Julie sighed. "Boy, are you weird."

"Whatever," I said. "So what about this John Wollman III?"

Greg and I both leaned in closer. We were the perfect audience for Julie.

"I emailed him," she said. "And he emailed back."

"But how did you find his email address?" Greg asked.

"Same way I did with the last ghost."

"Oh yeah," Greg said. "The Internet white pages or whatever."

"Anyway," Julie continued, "I couldn't be sure it was the right person, but since it was the same name, and he was the third, it all fit. Plus, Philadelphia. So I asked if he was related to a John Wollman who was an army medic during World War II."

"So what did he say?" I asked. I couldn't believe Julie was

stretching this out so long. The bell was going to ring any minute for class. Lunch period only lasts half an hour.

"He didn't *say* anything," Julie said. "He *emailed* me, though."

Now I was getting exasperated. Greg had this look on his face like he thought Julie was just being — I don't know exactly — maybe *charming*.

"And?" I said, trying to hide my irritation.

Just then the bell rang. We were out of time, and now we were going to have to wait until after school when we met up at the Kitchen Sink for band practice to hear the rest.

Julie paused when she stood up with her lunch tray. "And he wrote, 'Who wants to know?'"

·   ·   ·

I was standing at the urinal, doing my business, thinking I was totally alone in the bathroom, when somebody spoke.

"I didn't have any children. I wasn't ever even married."

I started to turn and see who it was — I hadn't heard anybody else come in — but, well, I couldn't.

"Uh, be with you in a second," I said over my shoulder as I finished up. "Just have to wash my hands."

But nobody was there.

"Ghost?" I said. "Is that you? I mean John. John Wollman. Is that you?"

It had to have been. And if it was, it meant that even if he was having a hard time showing himself, and sticking around for longer than a couple of seconds, he was at least able to be close enough — somewhere, somehow — to listen in on our conversations.

It also meant John Wollman III couldn't be his grandson.

CHAPTER 6

Julie and I were the first to the Kitchen Sink that afternoon for band practice. Greg was late, as usual. But it gave me a chance to tell her about the encounter in the restroom.

"He must have heard us talking," she said. "But you're right about him not having a grandson. There couldn't be a third if there wasn't a junior, and there couldn't be a junior if he never got married or had any kids."

"Right," I said. "So what do we do?"

"We wait for John Wollman III to email me back," she said. "Maybe he's still related to our John Wollman somehow. You never know."

I strummed through a chord progression on my electric guitar, even though I hadn't plugged it into my amplifier yet. "Why does this stuff always have to be so complicated?" I asked. "Wouldn't it be nice for once if we could solve one of these mysteries in just one day?"

"Well, certainly," Julie said. "But just think how difficult it must be for the ghost? You said it yourself. Corporal Wollman didn't even know he *was* a ghost, or at least that's how it sounded."

I nodded and kept strumming. I was the least musically talented of the three of us — Julie was by far the best, and Greg had really gotten a lot better on guitar, and could even play some lead guitar on some of our songs. But I was still trying to master barre chords. Plus, now I was the lead singer — ever since Greg's voice had started cracking — and it was making me very anxious. I actually had to leave the stage and throw up at the last open mic competition. Which we lost, though at least we didn't come in last. I did manage to come back on after Greg filled in on the first song, and I warbled my way on vocals through the rest of our three-song set.

"I'll tell you what else would be nice," I said. "And that's if John Wollman could stick around for a little while longer one of these times he shows up, or even if it's just his voice we hear, like in the bathroom."

"Well, here's his chance," Julie said, looking behind me.

"What do you mean?" I asked, but I kind of had a feeling as I turned.

John Wollman was sitting on Greg's amp. He smiled and waved. "Hey," he said, sounding almost shy.

Julie and I waved back, even though we were just ten feet away.

"Sorry for all the coming and going," John Wollman said. "I'm having a hard time getting used to, well, to this." He gestured at himself and then all around him. I nodded as if I knew what he meant, and maybe I did.

"Being around people?" Julie asked.

"Yes," he said. "And being around myself, as strange as I guess that must sound."

"We understand," Julie said. "We were just hoping you wouldn't disappear so quickly. We have so much to tell you, and to ask you."

"So we can help you," I added.

He thanked us. "I already heard you say my name. John Wollman. Or Corporal Wollman. But I hope you'll just call me John. Or Johnny. That's what they called me when I was little."

"But there's no John or Johnny Jr.?" Julie asked. "Or the third?"

"Nope," he said. "None that I know of."

"Well, I emailed one, in Philadelphia," she said. "I sort of explained who we thought you were and I'm hoping he'll email me back with more information."

John just blinked at us for a minute, then said, "Email?"

"It's just a new kind of mail," I said. "Only a lot faster than the mail you know about."

"Okay," he said. "Well, I'll be curious to hear what you find out. You know I used to live in Philadelphia."

"We were hoping so," Julie said. "That's what's on your ID card. Or that's where they inducted you into the army."

"Medical corps," John said. "I do remember that."

"And do you remember North Africa?" I asked. "You said something about that yesterday, and Greg and I have been doing a lot of research about the war in North Africa."

Julie laughed. "What Anderson means is that Greg's dad told him a lot about the start of the war, and about North Africa, and Greg told it to Anderson."

"It's still research," I said defensively. "Greg took notes."

Now John laughed. "You two sound like a couple of kids."

Julie sat up as tall as she could. "We're in middle school," she said.

"And we have our own band," I added, though saying that probably made us sound more like kids — like little kids — than if I hadn't said anything.

"It's okay," John said, still laughing. "I always liked kids. Heck, it wasn't that long ago that I was a kid myself."

"Uh, how old do you think you are, John?" I asked. "I mean, how old *are* you?"

"Twenty," he said. "Or I was, whenever I guess I stopped being anything." He looked upset. The smile vanished. He wasn't laughing anymore.

"I found out that you went missing — actually absent without leave is what they wrote officially," Julie said. "Do you remember anything about that?"

John didn't answer, just shook his head.

"We're sorry," Julie said. "I know this has to be really hard for you."

John rubbed his eyes as if he might start crying. The dirt and smoke on his face were smudged when he took his hands away. "It's okay," he said. "I don't mean to make you kids feel low about all of this. Anyway, I appreciate you helping me. And reaching out to me."

"It's been seventy years since the war ended," Julie said quietly. "Did you know that?"

John teared up again. He couldn't seem to speak so just shook his head.

We heard footsteps on the stairs coming down to the basement, and Greg humming a song I'd never heard before.

"Your friend is here," John said. "You all have your band practice, so I'd better go."

"Oh, don't," Julie said. "We have so much more to talk about."

"Hey!" Greg said, bounding through the door. "Sorry I'm late."

"I'll be back," John said, but his voice already sounded like it was coming from really far away, which I guess it was because when I looked at him again, he was gone and there was nothing — and no one — left to see.

Julie started crying, too. Greg saw it before I did, and went over to her right away and took off his beanie and even put his arm around her. She buried her face in his shirt and kept crying. Greg had a sad look on his face, even though he'd missed everything that had just happened. He shrugged at me and patted Julie on her back. I kept quiet.

It took a lot longer than I thought it would for Julie to come back to us. I didn't know if she was still crying that whole time, or just didn't want us to see her face all red and splotchy the way some people's faces get, or whether she just felt awkward and embarrassed that she was crying into Greg's shirt and they were hugging — which I'm pretty sure is how I would have felt.

Finally, Greg patted her again and said, "Uh, Julie, are you okay?"

She pulled her face a little bit away from him and nodded, but didn't look up.

I asked if she wanted me to go find a tissue and she shook her head no.

"Is it because you wiped your nose on Greg's shirt?" I asked.

She hesitated, and then nodded again.

Greg said, "Ew. Gross."

There was silence for a second, and then Julie couldn't help it — she burst out laughing, and that did it for me and Greg. We started laughing, too.

"Disgusting," I said.

"Revolting," Greg added. I didn't know he even knew the word.

Julie responded by actually wiping her nose on Greg's shirt again and then we totally lost it. It's weird, and I can't explain it, but I guess sometimes when you're the saddest, that's when dumb things like snot on a T-shirt are the funniest.

Julie even told a joke. "How do you make a tissue dance?"

She didn't even wait for us to say we didn't know.

"You put a little boogie in it!"

I would have run home and changed my shirt, but Greg didn't seem to care, and once Julie got it together, we actually ended up practicing for the next hour. We didn't talk about John again that afternoon, but I had a feeling he was still somewhere close by, and I hoped he enjoyed the music. I sang as well as I could, and I was pretty sure Julie and Greg had never played better.

CHAPTER 7

Julie checked her phone for email messages as we were leaving.

"I got another response!" she said. "From the guy. From John Wollman III!"

Uncle Dex had already left, so we stopped at the front desk while Julie read the email.

"Hmmm," she said.

"What?" Greg asked. "Why 'Hmmm'?"

" 'Hmmm' because all he wrote me back was 'What's it worth?' "

"The medic's kit?" I asked.

She nodded. "I told him who we were, and that we found it at your uncle's store, and that it had John Wollman's ID, and everything — except about us meeting John, of course, or his ghost. I couldn't tell him that. But I said we wanted to return the kit to his family and asked if he wanted it."

"So we still don't know for sure if the John Wollman III who wrote this email is related to our John Wollman?" Greg asked.

"I guess not," said Julie. "You'd think he'd at least be interested in something besides if he can make some money by selling it or whatever."

"Yeah," I said. "That's probably why he asked, I guess. So what do we do now? Everybody else was always so nice when we got in touch with them for our other ghosts. All their families and their old friends."

We were stumped until Greg spoke up. "He could just be having a rough day and we caught him at a bad time. Or he just lost his job or something. Maybe that's why he's thinking about whether there's some money in it for him. Maybe we should try him again. Give him another chance."

"Okay," Julie said. "I'm going to email him back and ask him again." She started tapping on the keys on her phone.

"We don't know what it's worth. We just need to know if you are the right relative. That's all." She clicked send.

"I bet there's a ton of these around," Greg said. "I bet it's not worth anything."

"Doesn't matter," Julie replied. "As long as he thinks maybe he can get something for it, he'll email us back and we can find out if he's who we're looking for. I would like to keep it. But if he's family, then we owe it to him to let him have the bag."

"I bet he's not going to help us," I said.

"Yeah," said Greg, "but maybe there's some other family member who will help."

"If he's even the right guy," I said. "Remember, John said he didn't have any kids."

"Well, I hope we find out one way or the other," Julie said. "But, meanwhile, we need to keep doing our research. I'm going to do more searching online for other possible relatives. And I'll check out some Internet sites and go to the library to find some books on the army and the medical corps and the war in North Africa. You guys need to do more reading, too."

"Hey," said Greg. "I already found out most of what we know."

"From your dad," I said.

"Still counts," he said.

Julie and I both said, "Whatever."

· · ·

We rode our bikes together for a couple of blocks, still debating whether Greg finding out stuff from his dad counted as research.

"It's interviewing," Greg argued. "And interviewing is research. It's, um, what do you call it?"

"A primary source," Julie said.

Greg grinned. "Right! A primary source. That's the best kind of source, isn't it?"

"Yes," Julie said, as if she was the great authority on the subject. Which, of the three of us, she probably was. "As long as you can verify what your source tells you."

"Verify?" Greg asked.

"Make sure it's true," I said.

"And how do you do that?" Greg asked.

I laughed. "From another source, dummy."

"No," Julie corrected me. "From an authoritative source. Anybody can be a source, but that doesn't mean they know what they're talking about. You have to make sure they're an expert, or an eyewitness or something."

"I doubt my dad was an eyewitness to World War II," Greg said. "He might be old, but he wasn't even born then."

"So, like I said, boys," Julie finished, "more research."

She veered away from us, taking a right turn just as we got to the Masonic cemetery, which was a lucky thing because just then there was a loud *pop* and something flew over the cemetery wall. It hit the side of my bike, splattering some kind of goo all over me. Some hit Greg, too.

"Oh my gosh!" Julie yelled, racing back over. "What is that?"

Fortunately, whatever hit us hadn't hurt or done any damage. It was just messy.

Greg scooped some up and sniffed it. "Yuck," he said. "Rotten potato."

We heard laughter coming from the other side of the wall, so we threw down our bikes and ran over, but by the time we got there, whoever had done it was already disappearing around a building on the other side of the cemetery.

I was pretty sure I recognized them, though.

Greg did, too.

"Belman!" He practically spit the name. And then he surprised me by actually vaulting over the stone wall. By the time I got over, too, he was kneeling in the grass between a couple of ancient headstones.

"I knew it!" he said, pointing. "Rotten potatoes." He stuck his finger in one and pulled it out. "The skin is just firm enough to hold it together."

"At least it wasn't a rubber chicken this time," Julie said, which surprised me since she was the one who usually got the most outraged over stuff like this, not the one doing the comic relief.

"I bet they have a potato cannon," she said.

"You're joking, right?" I said.

"No, they're real," Julie replied. "They're homemade cannons. You use a length of PVC pipe, and hair spray, and some kind of ignition switch. They're very dangerous."

"Dangerous to the person who gets hit by the rubber chicken," Greg said sullenly.

"And the person who gets hit by the potato," I added.

"Well, that, too," Julie said. "But I meant dangerous to the person shooting the potato cannon. Because it could blow up in their hand if they use too much hair spray, or make it incorrectly, or light it wrong. All kinds of ways it's dangerous. So we should turn them in — Belman and his Three Stooges. It would be for their own good."

Greg and I looked at each other with alarm. "Turn in Belman?" Greg asked. "That's crazy. First, nobody would believe us, and second, Belman and the Stooges would kill us."

"We can't just let them get away with something like this. And what if they'd hit you guys in the eye? What then?" Julie demanded, hands on her hips, clearly exasperated.

"Uh, it might have blinded us?" Greg asked.

"Exactly," said Julie. "And that's just what I'm talking about."

"Blindness?" I asked.

"Ratting out Belman?" Greg said.

"No," said Julie. "Finding a way to get back at Belman."

"You mean revenge?" Greg asked.

Julie nodded, a very serious look on her face. "Exactly."

CHAPTER 8

Later that night, all three of us did research at our various houses — a lot of reading, and a lot of texting back and forth with different things we found out.

Did you know that at the start of World War II we only had the seventeenth largest army in the world? Greg texted.

Yes, Julie wrote back, because of course she already knew everything before anybody else. *Right behind Romania!*

No way, Greg wrote. *Romania's army was bigger than ours?*

What about North Africa? I texted. *Anybody gotten to that yet?*

Yes, wrote Julie. *Of course. And get this — when we first invaded North Africa — in Morocco and Algeria — we weren't fighting the Germans or the Italians. We were fighting the French!*

Yeah, Greg texted. *Anderson and I kind of figured that out. The Vichy French, actually.*

Did you guys get the date for the invasion? I wrote. *November 8, 1942.*

The British were with us, I added. *Don't forget them. They were part of the invasion. Plus, they were already in North Africa. Over in Egypt and Libya. They'd been fighting off the Italians and Germans there for two years already.*

Right, Julie wrote. *The French were on the Atlantic Ocean side of North Africa. We sent this huge fleet across the Atlantic, and another fleet from England, and we landed in Morocco and Algeria and pretty much surprised the French. We defeated them quickly. In just three days. It was all over by November 10. Plus, they wanted to be on our side, anyway, and as soon as they saw they couldn't stop us, they surrendered and joined us and the British.*

Yay for us! I wrote.

It wasn't just some party, Julie replied. *Or a picnic. A lot of soldiers got killed just in those three days. And that was only the beginning.* I could practically hear the scolding in her text.

The texts continued for a while longer, but fewer of them, and longer apart, until finally we all admitted we were too tired to read any more and were all heading for bed.

I sent one last text. *Any word yet from John Wolman III?*

Julie sent back a one-word response. *No.*

• • •

I had just turned off the light and crawled into bed when the original John Wollman showed up. I should have been expecting him with all the things we were learning, all the energy or whatever that Julie and Greg and I had been generating all night trying to solve the mystery.

He stood quietly just inside my bedroom door. Moonlight poured in through an opening in the curtains, right on him, but he didn't cast a shadow.

"Sorry I broke down on you and your friends earlier," he said. "I heard you playing your songs afterward. Sounded really nice."

"Thanks," I said. "And it's okay. About breaking down, I mean."

He nodded, and then changed the subject.

"We didn't think we would actually have to fight the French," he said. "I do remember that. Even when we were on the landing craft, coming off the ships and heading to shore, everybody thought they would be happy to see us."

"So you were in, like, the first wave of the attack?" I asked. "In North Africa?"

"It was a beach in Algeria," he said. "Funny how things come back to you like that. I can remember it now. And I can remember how dumb we were about what was going to happen. Even though the officers kept telling us to be ready to fight. But nobody believed the French would fire on us like they did. We thought they'd just want to know what took us so long to get there, and give us wine, and have marching bands."

"Wow," I said. "Sounds like a lot of it's coming back to you."

"Flashes of it, anyway," he said. "Like the name you told me, from the ID badge — John Wollman. That sounds right, that it's my name, but at the same time it sounds like you're talking about somebody else. Somebody I used to know, or used to be, a really long time ago."

I said I thought that made sense, and I asked him what other flashes he had besides being on the landing craft and waiting for the big party with the French once they landed on the beach in Algeria.

He looked away from me, toward that big moon outside. "I remember the first guy," he said, his voice much softer, not that he'd been loud before.

"They started firing on us before we made it to the beach. And they kept it up once we landed. Everybody was scrambling to find cover, but it was already too late for a lot of guys. Some went straight down in the water and never came back up. Others dropped to the sand as soon as they set foot on land. And they didn't get up, either."

He paused. "There was one. He was right in front of me. There was an explosion. It must have been a land mine that he stepped on. His leg, or most of his leg, was just gone. He was screaming and screaming and I knew I was supposed to help him. It was my job. I was a medic. And guys around him were yelling for me. 'Medic! Medic!' But I froze. And like an idiot, I just stood there. Bullets and bombs all around, and there I was like a statue. Couldn't move. Couldn't make myself do anything. I don't know how I didn't get hit, too. But there he was, this poor soldier, his leg blown off just above the knee, and blood pouring out of an artery. He was flopping from side to side and screaming."

John paused again.

"So what did you do?" I asked.

"I guess all the training took over, because I started doing things I didn't know I could make myself do. I got down on my knees beside him and pulled back his ripped pant leg, and I leaned on his leg with my stomach to try to slow down the bleeding while I tore off part of his pants to make a tourniquet. I didn't even have time to get my own tourniquet kit out of my medical pouch. He would have probably bled out by the time I found it.

"Once I got the tourniquet tied on and cinched as tight as I could get it, then I could dig through my pouch for some morphine. That's what we had to give them, to deaden the pain. I gave him a shot right in his abdomen, and as soon as that started to work on him, I had to get my biggest needle out and sew up the leg as best I could. I just hoped I could reach the artery and suture that, too, but I really couldn't tell if I did or not. But it was all I could do. Then I poured on the sulfa powder and the biggest bandage I had. That was hard to tape down because of how slippery the stump of his leg was from all the blood. But finally I got it on."

"Were you able to save him?" I asked.

John sighed. "Don't know. I hope so. Anyway, he was still alive when they came with a litter to put him on it and carry him off the beach. I guess they'd been able to set up a surgical tent by then in a safe spot. Things were happening so fast I couldn't be sure where they took him. And there were so many other men that needed help. So I had to leave him and just keep going. To the next guy. And the next guy. And the next guy."

"So you never saw him again?" I asked.

"No," John said. "He was passed out. From losing all that blood, and his leg, or from the morphine. Or from the shock. Anyway, he was my first. I said a prayer for him while they carried him off. And I thought about him every day after that, hoping he lived. Or I guess I should say I thought about him every day that I was still alive myself."

CHAPTER 9

I asked John if he remembered anything else about that day. He frowned and brought his hands together under his chin, almost as if he was saying a prayer right then.

"I remember what happened before that. I remember the ocean when we were on the landing craft," he said. "I remember climbing down the side of the ship to board, and how rough the waves were, and guys asking me for something to keep them from getting seasick. But I didn't have anything. So a bunch of them, you know, lost their dinner right there in the landing craft, which was pretty disgusting, and everybody stepped in it because there wasn't anywhere else to stand until we hit the beach, or close enough to the beach that we were supposed to be able to wade to shore."

"And then the land mine," I said. "And the guy lost his leg."

John nodded. "Yeah. And then that happened. But I don't remember much after that. Just that there were more guys, and they kept calling for me — 'Medic!' Or I guess calling for any of us in the medical corps who were close enough to help."

John had been around a lot longer this time than ever before, but, of course, as soon as I thought about that, wouldn't you know he started fading out again, going all staticky so I couldn't understand what else he was saying. And then he was gone.

.　.　.

I woke up in the morning humming a song I'd never heard before. Actually, I wasn't even aware that I was humming it until I walked into the kitchen to get breakfast. Mom was at the table, drinking a cup of coffee and reading the newspaper, just like an ordinary parent and not like the one she usually was — the one with MS, and having to stay in her bed most of the time.

"Hi, sweetheart," she said. "Want some coffee?"

I knew she wasn't serious — they would never let me drink coffee — but I said sure anyway, hoping she'd let me just for once this morning. I probably hadn't gotten five hours' worth of sleep.

To my surprise, she got up and went over to the coffeepot and poured some in a mug. Then she poured about four times as much milk in with it, and stirred in some sugar. "Don't tell your dad," she said. "And it's just this once."

I thanked her, but probably should have said, "No thanks," instead, because even with the milk and the sugar, it tasted bitter, like something somebody burned. I couldn't imagine what it would have tasted like *without* the sugar and milk.

Mom laughed. "Not a fan?"

She didn't wait for an answer, just grabbed a box of cereal and poured me a bowl, with some milk. I ate as fast as I could — less because I was hungry than because I wanted to get the nasty taste out of my mouth.

Mom sat with me while I shoveled it in. "I didn't know you knew that song," she said.

I looked up with what I'm sure was a quizzical look on my face. "What song?"

"The one you were humming when you came in," she said. "Don't you remember?"

I shook my head.

She started singing. "'Tis the gift to be simple, 'tis the gift to be free, 'tis the gift to come down where we ought to be . . ."

I recognized it right away, sort of. And realized I *had* been humming it. But I still had no idea where I'd ever heard it before.

"It's an old song that the Quakers like to sing," she said. "It's called 'Simple Gifts.' I've always loved that song."

I had to admit it was really pretty. But I was still confused about why I'd been humming it.

"You do know who the Quakers are, don't you?" Mom asked.

I nodded. "Oh, sure. We studied them in school, too. They were a religious group. Kind of a small religious group, one of those that came over from Europe so they could practice their religion the way they wanted. But that's about all I know."

"That's right," Mom said. "They're a small religion with very different beliefs than the mainstream churches. There aren't a lot of Quakers, but some still practice it today. Especially up in Pennsylvania — around Philadelphia — in that area."

"What do they believe?" I asked. The mention of Philadelphia definitely had me interested, since that was where John Wollman was from.

"Oh, well, let's see. They won't go to war, or they won't fight in wars, anyway. And they believe in living very simply, and helping other people, especially prisoners, and anyone suffering from war, or poverty, or anything like that." Mom took another sip of her coffee and carefully folded the newspaper. "As I understand it, they believe that God is in each person, and God shows Himself to ordinary people directly. So they don't really have ministers or priests or anyone who is in charge. They call themselves the Society of Friends, because everyone is equal, and whoever feels called to can speak at their meetings. Or they just sit quietly. At many of their Friends meetings, no one says anything at all. Not like our church."

We're Presbyterians, and Mom was definitely right about that — it didn't sound anything at all like what I was used to at Sunday school and church, where we sat in pews and sang hymns and listened to Bible readings and a twenty-minute sermon, which if it runs any longer than that people start checking their watches, wondering what's up with the minister.

"And you said they don't believe in war?" I asked. "So what about when there *is* a war? Like, um, World War II? What would they do then, like if they were drafted or whatever?"

Mom shrugged. "I guess some sort of alternative service."

"Like what?"

"Oh, I don't know," Mom said. "I'm certainly no expert. But my guess would be that they would serve as doctors or nurses or orderlies, that sort of thing. Helping people who are wounded."

"You mean like a medic?" I asked, practically shouting.

Mom laughed at how excited I was. "Why, yes," she said. "I suppose so."

"Cool. Thanks, Mom," I said, grabbing my backpack and dashing out of the kitchen and out to the garage for my bike. "I've got to go — going to be late for school."

I couldn't wait to tell Julie and Greg — and John! This

was huge. Another major clue to share. I must have picked up the song from him somehow. Maybe he came back in my bedroom and sang it in the middle of the night while I was dead asleep. Maybe he'd been humming it under his breath all along without me even noticing. Who knows?

CHAPTER 10

Julie had news, too, and she
started telling us before I had a chance to tell them mine.
She'd gotten a message back from John Wollman III.

"He said never mind about the medic's pouch. He said
he didn't guess he needed it and thanks anyway," she said. I
had just joined her and Greg outside the school. We still had
a few minutes before the homeroom bell.

"Well, where does that leave us?" I asked. "I mean,
what now?"

"We need fifty dollars," Julie said. "That's what."

"Why?" Greg asked.

"I wrote him back again," Julie said. "I explained that since we found the medic's pouch and John Wollman's ID, that we decided to do a research project for school about him and the war in North Africa and the medical corps, and was there anything he could tell us to help us find out if *our* John Wollman was also *his* John Wollman, and if there was anything he could also tell us about who *our* — and hopefully *his* — John Wollman was."

"That's very complicated," Greg said. "So did he answer?"

Julie nodded. "He said John Wollman had been his great-uncle, and that he had a stash of letters that John Wollman wrote during the war. He offered to sell them to us for a hundred dollars."

"That's great!" I said. "I mean about him having the letters. But why can't he just send us copies of them and not charge us anything?"

"Yeah. Where are we going to come up with fifty dollars?" Greg asked. "I don't have that kind of money."

"Me neither," I said. I was concerned about something else, too. "Did you tell your parents about this?"

Julie looked annoyed. "Of course I did," she said. "My mom even helped me."

"Helped you how?" Greg asked.

Julie smiled. "Negotiate. He wanted a hundred, but she emailed him and got him down to fifty. She said if it was that important to me for our research project I could buy the letters — but John Wollman III can only get the money after he sends them to us."

"Wow," I said. "Your mom is awesome."

"I know," Julie said. "And you don't have to worry about the money. I have some from my birthday that I didn't spend yet. So now we just have to wait."

The bell rang and we all dashed off for homeroom. I realized there'd been so much going on that I still hadn't told them my news.

•   •   •

I took care of that at lunch — told them all about the army landing in Algeria, and John Wollman's first casualty he treated, and about me waking up humming "Simple Gifts," and about everything Mom had told me about the Quakers. They were pretty impressed with what I'd found out, too. "I can't wait to tell him," I said. "I bet just knowing about him being a Quaker will bring back some memories about stuff."

"Yeah, probably," said Greg. But then he switched the conversation back over to John Wollman III. "It's those letters I'm mostly interested in. I really, really can't wait to see what's in there."

"I wonder why John Wollman III isn't interested in the medic's pouch, or in anything else about his great-uncle. He just seems to want to find a way to make money," I said.

"Well, maybe it's like Greg said yesterday," Julie responded. "Maybe he just lost his job, or just really needs money right now for some other reason. We shouldn't judge him without knowing."

"Well, I'd still be interested in finding out about my great-uncle and what he did in the war," I said. "No matter what. So it's hard not to judge the guy."

A chair scraped out from the table next to Julie and somebody sat down, interrupting our conversation. It was Belman, of course, though no Three Stooges with him for once.

"And who might that be?" he asked. He had his usual smirk on. "The guy you're going to judge? Were you little potato heads talking about me?"

Julie tensed up. I tried being sarcastic. "Oh yeah, sure, Belman. Because we don't have anything better to do with our time than to talk about you."

The sarcasm was lost on him, though. "I thought so," he said. "Well, sorry to disappoint you little spudnuts, but I really couldn't care less." He grabbed a bag of chips from Julie's lunch box. "Just dropped by for a snack."

He was gone before any of us could stop him.

"Did you hear that?" Greg asked, fuming. "He called us potato heads and spudnuts. So it was definitely him and his friends who blasted us with those rotten potatoes yesterday. Or why else would he say that?"

Julie clenched her fists. "One of these days," she said, "we're getting that guy back. One way or another."

. . .

I was in the bathroom that afternoon when I heard somebody humming "Simple Gifts." This time it wasn't me.

"John?" I asked from inside the stall. "Is that you?"

It was the second time he'd shown up in the bathroom. I wondered if he'd stick around a little longer this time.

"Yes," he said. "Out here waiting. You going to be long in there?"

"Uh, not much longer," I said. "Is anybody else out there?" I couldn't imagine there would be.

"Nope," John said. "Just me. Hope you don't mind me

showing up here. It's about the only place there's any privacy."

"Oh, it's not the first time a ghost has followed me into the bathroom at school," I said.

I finished up quickly and came out of the stall to wash my hands. John was leaning against the wall under a high window.

"I couldn't help overhearing some of your conversation at lunch," he said.

"What part?"

"About a brother. My brother. And that he named his son after me. So there's a John Wollman III now, too."

"Do you remember all that?" I asked. "About having a brother and being from Philadelphia? And were you — are you — a Quaker?"

John looked surprised. "A Quaker?"

"Uh, I think they call it the Society of Friends," I said. "You were humming one of their songs just now. I was humming it, too, this morning when I woke up. I must have heard it from you. My mom knows the words."

He smiled and sang softly, the same lyrics my mom had sung that morning at breakfast. "'Tis the gift to be simple, 'tis the gift to be free . . ."

"That's it," I said.

"I guess I do remember," John said. "At least I remember that. And come to think of it I do remember my brother! His name was Aaron. He was my little brother — too young to get drafted." He laughed. "I remember Aaron and I always had a hard time sitting quiet in the Friends meetings the way we were supposed to. But nobody got on us about it, of course — about squirming and messing with each other. That wasn't the Friends way."

His smile faded. "I wonder if he's still alive. It's been a long, long time since then, and since I went off to the war. I sure would love to see him again."

CHAPTER 11

Julie, or her mom, got another email from John Wollman III, telling us it was going to take him a couple of days to mail us the letters since he was going to have to go across town to get them out of a storage unit. He also told them, because Julie and her mom had asked, that John Wollman's brother, Aaron, had died a long time ago. Aaron's son, John Wollman Jr., had passed away, too, a couple of years ago. So had his wife. If there was any other family, John Wollman III didn't mention them. He must have read the letters, though, or heard stories about his great-uncle, because he warned us about something.

Good luck writing your school paper about the guy.
He was a pacifist in World War II, which a lot of
people back then thought was just a big excuse for
cowards getting out of going to war. Plus, they said he
went AWOL in the middle of the war and no one ever
saw him again. That's not exactly what makes for a
brave soldier.

"Wow," Greg said. "That was mean. Maybe John Wollman III is just a big jerk after all."

"I thought we weren't supposed to judge him," I said.

Julie ignored us. "The important thing is we're getting the letters. And we've learned a lot already. We know John's name, and his brother's name, and they were Quakers from Philadelphia. And of course we know John was a medic, and he served in the army in the war in North Africa."

"We know he landed in Algeria," I added. "And they had to fight the French army there. At least for a couple of days."

"But we still don't know what happened to him," Greg said. "How he ended up AWOL — and missing."

"Maybe there will be something in the letters," Julie said. "And maybe just what we know already will be enough to help John remember more things the next time he shows up. We can ask him about being a pacifist."

"A lot of Quakers were," I said. "So it makes sense. They didn't believe in war, but they believed in helping people."

"Right," Greg said. "And you know what I would like to tell that John Wollman III? That I bet it took a lot of guts to be out there on that beach trying to save the guy who lost his leg. Maybe even more guts than if he'd been shooting a gun or whatever. He must have been getting shot at, too, the same as all the rest of the soldiers, even if he was a pacifist."

"Conscientious objector," Julie said. "That's what they called them. It meant they objected to the war, that it was against their religion, or their conscience."

"Do you guys ever wonder what you would do?" I asked. "Or what you would have done? If you would have gone to fight like you were ordered to do. Like in World War II. Or if you would have been a, um, what Julie said."

"A conscientious objector," she repeated.

"Right," I said. "That. But, anyway, do you guys wonder about that?"

Greg shrugged. "I would have gone to fight," he said, not even having to think about it. "My dad did. I would have, too. But knowing what I know from what the ghosts have told us, I wouldn't have thought about it the way I used to."

"Which was how?" I asked.

"Oh, you know," he said. "Like it's a video game. Call of Duty. Something like that. Or like in the movies. It just seems so much more real now. And so much sadder than I ever thought. Even though I already knew how it affected my dad."

Julie nodded with a solemn face. "I feel that way, too. Only I think perhaps I would be a conscientious objector. Depending on the war. Though I'm not sure that's how it works. I suppose you can be against war because of your religion, but you would have to be against all war. Like John Wollman. Or at least that's what we think was the case with him. But that's where it gets complicated, because some wars I think maybe you do have to fight. So maybe I don't know what I would do. I know I'd be very afraid. And like Greg, I know now that it would be very sad for the families."

I didn't have to tell them what I thought — which was a good thing, since I didn't *know* what I thought — because John Wollman showed up just then. We were in our basement practice room, supposedly having band practice, though we hadn't quite gotten to that yet. And it would be a while longer before we picked up our instruments.

"Hey, kids," John said. He looked around the dusty room, his gaze pausing on the footlocker in the corner, where we'd found his medic pouch. "Much better meeting you guys in here than where I ran into Anderson earlier."

"He means the bathroom at school," I explained.

"Oh, definitely," Greg said, laughing.

"Anything new in the investigation?" John asked. "I had a feeling maybe there was something."

Julie told him about the letters that were on the way in the mail. She left it for me to tell him that his brother, Aaron, had passed away a long time ago, and as far as we knew, there was just the one living relative — John Wollman III.

"Who is a big jerk," Greg blurted out.

John looked at him expectantly. "Oh?"

"Sorry," Greg said. "I shouldn't have said that."

"It's okay," John replied. He was standing close to Greg and lifted his hand as if he was going to pat Greg on the back, or give him a hug.

Julie read him the email from John Wollman III, including the part about people thinking pacifists were cowards.

"We don't think that," Julie quickly assured him. "Not at all."

"We think you were really brave," I added. "Out there on that beach in the middle of the landing, and doing what you did to save that guy. And all the other guys you saved."

"*Tried* to save," John corrected me. "I couldn't say if I did or didn't. And, anyway, not much bravery in that. I don't remember ever thinking I was brave. Just really, really scared. Scared once we climbed off the ship onto the landing craft. Scared when we landed. Scared tending to those boys that got wounded. Scared so bad I didn't ever stop being scared."

"But you still did your job," Greg says. "That's what it sounds like. And I bet my dad would say that's the same thing as being brave."

"Your dad a veteran?" John asked, still looking like he thought Greg needed a hug. I thought it was John Wollman who needed the hug. But there's no way you can hug a ghost, of course.

"Yeah," Greg replied.

John got a funny, faraway look for a couple of very quiet minutes.

"When I was in training, I heard it a lot," he said finally. "About what a coward I was that I wouldn't fight. One drill instructor, he made a sport out of trying to get me to fight, to defend myself. Calling me names. Saying things about my family. About my mom especially. That was hard. Hard not to retaliate. I'm still not sure how I managed to keep from doing, well, something. And it was other guys, too. I kept reminding myself what Jesus said about turning the other cheek. What I had always been taught my whole life growing up. One time I did make a fist. That drill instructor spit on my uniform. I don't know if he meant to or he was just so worked up about what a gutless coward he said I was, and the spit just accidentally sprayed out. Either way, I almost couldn't help myself. I even drew my arm back to hit him."

Greg was beside himself with anticipation and anger on John's behalf, or that's how it looked to me, anyway. "And did you?" he asked. "Did you finally hit him? Because it sure sounds like he deserved it."

John smiled and shook his head. "No. My mom wouldn't have liked that, and she had a way of finding out every-thing that happened. I'd probably have had to confess it to her in a letter. Not to mention they'd probably throw me in the stockade for something like that. So no, I let that one go, too."

"Did it continue?" Julie asked. "After you were in North Africa and saving lives. Did it continue?"

"Not with most guys," John said. "Once things got going, everybody was too busy trying to stay alive to worry too much about anybody else's business. Or almost everybody."

He seemed to be remembering something, or someone, but he started flickering out before he could say anything more, and once again, we were left leaning forward, waiting to find out what else there was.

CHAPTER 12

While we waited for the letters, we got back to work learning more about the war in North Africa. And there was plenty to learn. We went to the library and checked out a bunch of world atlases and World War II photo books and histories and timelines. One thing we kept getting confused about was the geography — at least Greg and I did. Julie, of course, had a photographic memory, so knowing which country went where on the map wasn't so much a problem for her. We finally figured out a way to remember, though: My Aunt Takes Licorice Everywhere. MATLE. I'm not exactly sure how we came up with that, other than the fact that Greg had sneaked in some Twizzlers and kept sticking his face in his backpack to munch on them so the librarians wouldn't see him since you're not supposed to have food in the library.

Anyway, MATLE are the initials for the countries of North Africa, starting on the Atlantic Ocean side and going east to the Red Sea.

Morocco, Algeria, Tunisia, Libya, and Egypt.

My Aunt Takes Licorice Everywhere.

Morocco, Algeria, and Tunisia were under the French, though there were tons of German and Italian troops in Tunisia.

Libya was under the Italians.

Egypt was with the British.

We already learned all that, but learning it and remembering it are two very different things.

We also learned (again) that from 1940 to 1942 the Italians and then the Germans attacked the British in Egypt. The Italians attacked first, but they had a lousy army so the British — and Australians — totally defeated them, and even captured one hundred and thirty thousand Italian soldiers in the process. Then the Germans had to go in and bail out the Italians, which Hitler wasn't too happy about.

A guy named General Bernard Montgomery led the British and Australian troops. A famous German general named Erwin Rommel led the Germans. They called Rommel the Desert Fox because he was such a great commander, usually able to outmaneuver the British, though not always. And this was the first time ever that war was waged using tanks to lead the way. So that made Rommel a pretty historic general. Montgomery had tanks, too — thousands of them supplied by America — but ours weren't as good as the Germans', which had stronger armor and were better engineered to go faster and shoot farther with greater power. They called Rommel's army the Afrika Korps.

Rommel's troops and Montgomery's troops fought these massive tank battles back and forth across Libya and Egypt through the desert — one side gaining ground and driving forward, then the other side counterattacking and pushing them back.

"And that's where we came in," Julie said. "November 1942."

I had to admit I was getting confused with so many countries and so many armies, so Julie offered to draw me a map of North Africa, with arrows showing me (and Greg, who was confused, too, but just didn't want to admit it) where the various armies started out and where they fought one another and where they ended up. Which was right in the middle of the continent.

"Tunisia," Julie said. "That was the place."

"So why did our troops land in Morocco and Algeria instead of there?" I asked, squinting at the lines that Julie had drawn.

"Because," she said, "when the Americans entered the war in 1941, there weren't any German or Italian troops in those two countries. Since it was just the French, we figured those would be the easiest places to occupy. And once we were there and the French switched to our side, we could take the war to the Germans and the Italians in Tunisia. Montgomery's tanks and troops had finally gained the upper hand and were pushing Rommel back to the west across Libya by that time, driving the Afrika Korps all the way into Tunisia."

I finally got it. "So if we trapped the Germans and Italians in Tunisia, we could attack from both sides, and from the south," I said, or asked.

"Right," said Julie. "And we could block German and Italian reinforcements and supplies from Europe in the north with our ships and planes in the Mediterranean."

Greg had been reading madly the whole time we talked. "They called it Operation TORCH," he announced.

"Cool name," I said.

"It looked like a great plan," Greg added. "At least on paper."

I agreed.

"All plans look good on paper," Julie said, sounding like she'd had a lot of experience with this sort of thing.

"So what are you saying?" I asked.

"Just keep reading and you'll see," she said.

·   ·   ·

In addition to General Montgomery and Rommel, the Desert Fox, we learned some other important names. First there was General Dwight Eisenhower, who was the commander in chief of the Allied armies. He was in charge of planning and then carrying out the invasion — and the rest of the war.

"And you know what else he was?" Julie quizzed us.

"Really tall?" Greg joked.

"Bald!" I added, laughing.

Julie shook her head. "The president, you morons. He was elected the president of the United States after the war. He served two terms. Hello?"

"I knew that," I said, because I actually did.

"Whatever," said Julie, probably not believing me at this point.

"And he really was bald," I added lamely.

"Yeah, and I'm pretty sure he was tall, too," Greg added.

"Back to work," Julie ordered.

Another name we found that was important — and of course we'd heard of him, too — was Franklin Roosevelt, who was president through most of the war. And then there was Winston Churchill, the British prime minister, who, during the Nazi bombing of London — which went on for months and months — said that famous line to encourage all the British citizens to be brave and to be strong: "We shall defend our island, whatever the cost may be, we shall fight on the beaches, we shall fight on the landing grounds, we shall fight in the fields and in the streets, we shall fight in the hills; we shall never surrender."

"I think that meant he believed there was no way the Nazis were going to win, no matter how many bombs they dropped and no matter how many people were killed," Greg said when we read it.

"That sounds about right," I said.

"Plus, he wanted to remind everybody that they couldn't

just hide," Julie said. "They had to not worry about the bombing and stay busy on the war effort."

Finally — well, not finally, because there were a lot of really important people involved in the war in North Africa and the rest of World War II, of course — but I guess the most important besides Eisenhower and Montgomery and Rommel and Roosevelt and Churchill was this guy Patton. Major General George Patton. He was probably the most famous American general of the war, and toward the end of the North Africa campaign, he was in charge of the American forces there. He was also what they called a glory hound — a guy who wanted all the credit for himself. Apparently there was a lot of that going around because we read that about the British general, Montgomery, too.

Besides being famous and a glory hound, Patton was supposed to be a great general, outmaneuvering and out-smarting and outgeneraling the enemy throughout the war. But, boy, was he also really weird.

"Hey, you guys," Greg said at one point, interrupting us from our reading. "I just read this thing about how one time Patton was mad at a soldier for not digging a foxhole deep enough, so he unzipped his pants and peed in the foxhole right in front of the soldier and everybody else around."

I burst out laughing.

"And there's more," Greg said. "Talk about a guy who liked to give orders. Even in the middle of the war, when men were fighting in mud and dust and the desert, he ordered that soldiers pay a fine of ten dollars if they weren't wearing their neckties as part of their uniforms."

"How hot do you think it got there?" I asked.

"Desert hot," Greg said.

Julie rolled her eyes.

All the accounts we read also said Patton was really brave. Or maybe foolish. Or both.

Once in Morocco enemy planes flew over Patton's head-quarters and opened up with machine guns, strafing buildings and tents and trucks, and sending soldiers scrambling for cover. Patton stormed outside with his service revolver and started cursing and shooting up at the planes until they left.

Greg and I thought that story was really cool, though neither one of us could imagine being that brave or that crazy to do what Patton did. "But I bet it totally inspired his men," Greg said. "Like that speech by Churchill did for the people in England."

"Probably so," I agreed. "Though it sure wouldn't have if he'd gotten killed."

Julie frowned. "First, that story about Patton shooting at the plane isn't true," she said. "It was in a movie about him, but they made it up. And second, after North Africa, when they were fighting in Italy, General Patton visited a hospital and one of the soldiers in the hospital didn't have any physical wounds. He had what they called shell shock, or combat fatigue. Today they call it post-traumatic stress. Soldiers who suffered from it just couldn't function anymore after they'd been in battles and seen their friends get killed, and had to kill people themselves. So sometimes they went into a kind of shock where they just cried and couldn't stop. Or they went numb and wouldn't speak to anybody and wouldn't move and couldn't follow orders. Didn't even seem to hear it when somebody gave them an order.

"So when General Patton met this one soldier in a military hospital who was that way, instead of understanding what the guy had been through and how it affected him, General Patton slapped the soldier and called him a coward for not being out fighting."

Greg and I both stared at Julie, horrified.

She continued, "Patton actually did that on two occasions, to two different soldiers with PTSD. He got in a lot of trouble for that. He had to apologize to all the troops, but they said you could tell from the way he gave his apology speech that he didn't mean it."

I felt deflated. Here I'd been thinking Patton was such a great leader, really cool and kind of over the top with the pistols and the peeing, but still great. And the books all said what a brilliant general he was, too, and how successful he'd been in North Africa, and later in the Italian campaign, and still later when the Allies liberated Europe and attacked Germany. But now, after what Julie had just told us, I almost didn't know what to think.

CHAPTER 13

When the letters didn't come
after a few days from John Wollman III, Julie emailed him again. It took another day to get a response, and it wasn't much. Just, *Oh yeah. I forgot to put them in the mail. I'll do that today.*

"Not even an 'I'm sorry' or anything," Julie said. We were at band practice and trying to focus on the set we would be playing at the next open mic competition, which would be our third one.

"I think we need a new song," Greg said. We had our standards — this antibullying song that Julie wrote, plus a song about hamsters that Julie also wrote. We'd gone back and forth on the third song.

"What about something a little different," Julie said, grinning. Clearly she had something in mind already.

"Like what?" I asked.

"Like rap," she said. "And I could do it. That way it wouldn't all have to be about you being the lead singer, with all the pressure and everything."

"Good call," Greg said. "And we all know what pressure can do to you, Anderson." He pretended to barf. I didn't think it was funny, but Julie did. I hated it when those two ganged up on me like that.

"So let's hear it," I said. "Your big rap number."

Julie shook her head. "I haven't exactly written it yet. But I will."

"Hey, I have an idea," Greg said. "Why don't you write it about Belman. You know, making fun of him or something. That can be how we get back at him for the rubber chicken and the potatoes."

"I have a better idea," I said. "Why don't we send an anonymous note to his parents and tell them about the potato cannon and get him in trouble."

Julie rolled her eyes. "And we can hold the rubber chicken for ransom while we're at it. I'm sure it's a family heirloom and they'll pay plenty to get it back."

Greg and I both knew she was making fun of us. Or I thought Greg and I both knew that. Then he said, "You know, that just might work. And that way we could get the money back that you spent paying John Wollman III for the letters!"

Julie turned back to her keyboard, not even bothering to respond, except to say, "Can we please just get back to practicing?"

· · ·

I was the last to leave that day. Something had been bothering me since reading about General Patton, but I couldn't quite put my finger on what it was. And then, sitting alone in the basement, messing around on my guitar, it hit me. I wanted war heroes to be just that — war heroes — and not anything else. I didn't want them to do mean things, too. Peeing in a foxhole, well, okay, I could live with that. It's a way to make a point, I guess, and it's funny.

But slapping a soldier who was suffering from a mental breakdown from being in battle — that wasn't something you did if you were a hero. That's something you did if you were a jerk. The problem was that apparently you could be both — a hero *and* a jerk. I'd thought we were the good guys in World War II, and we definitely were. Somebody had to stand up to Hitler and all the horrible, horrible things he did, and we were that somebody. But people like Patton still did such lousy things sometimes. It just didn't add up the way it was supposed to — or the way I wanted it to.

And then there was the other side. The way the books we read talked about the German general Rommel made him sound like a hero, too, which was strange. I mean, what a cool name they gave him — the Desert Fox. He was supposed to be this guy who had high principles and didn't think you should hate the people you were fighting, and he believed that it wasn't right to treat prisoners bad, or to follow Hitler's orders about killing Jewish people. In fact, he supposedly hated Hitler. He might have even been involved in a plot that attempted to assassinate Hitler later in the war, and then when the plot was discovered, he was forced to take his own life. So there was all that.

But at the same time Rommel was one of the greatest German generals, fighting for Hitler — or for Germany, anyway, but still taking his orders from Hitler. The American and British generals all seemed to respect him, but his Afrika Korps and the German tanks (panzers) led the way in killing thousands — tens of thousands — of our men.

Trying to make sense of it all made my head hurt. I sat

there in the Kitchen Sink basement a little while longer, strumming my guitar, until I realized what I was playing without even knowing it: that Quaker song, "Simple Gifts."

I still didn't know the words, so I just quietly hummed along with the chords until I felt better.

• • •

Uncle Dex was still working, so I stopped to talk to him, even though it was late and I should have already been home.

"Practice going well?" he asked.

"I don't know," I said. "Maybe. Probably not. We need to learn another song. Julie says she's going to write a rap song."

Uncle Dex immediately started beat boxing, or what he must have thought sounded like beat boxing, making this spitting noise into his fist or something. He was such a dork. It made me laugh.

"And how's the research going?" he asked when he finished.

"Research?" I repeated.

"Your soldier, the medic," he said. "I figured from the way you were all so interested in the medic's pouch and his identification card you were off on another research project, trying to learn about another ghost of war."

I nearly choked. "Ghost of war? Uh, there's no such thing as ghosts, Uncle Dex. I mean, really."

It was his turn to laugh. "It's just an expression. Or a band name," he said, though from the way he looked at me, as if studying my reaction, I had to wonder what he was really thinking.

"We're kind of stuck, actually," I said. "I mean, you're right, we are researching him. And we even found one of his relatives, his great-nephew, who lives in Philadelphia. We're pretty sure he was a Quaker. And he fought in North Africa in World War II. Well, he didn't fight exactly, but he took care of the guys who did the fighting."

Uncle Dex nodded. "That's quite a lot right there. Good work so far."

"The relative, he's sending us some of John Wollman's letters from when he was in the war. So far, though, we don't know what happened to him, and we're trying to figure that out. We're also trying to learn as much as we can about the war in North Africa. Like, I didn't even know we fought the French in North Africa. Did you know that?"

Uncle Dex nodded. "I might have heard a little something about that." The way he said it meant that he actually knew a lot about it, of course. I was prepared for him to launch into a long lecture, but instead he made a suggestion.

"You know who would be good to talk to," he said, "is Reverend Simpson. He fought in World War II and I'm pretty sure he took part in the North Africa campaign."

Reverend Earl Simpson used to be the mayor of Fredericksburg. He was also a minister at one of the churches in town — Bethel Baptist. Everybody knew about him because he had served four terms as mayor, starting out during the civil rights years back in the 1970s. Apparently it was pretty unusual for a town back then in the South, like ours, to elect a black mayor. He wasn't a town political leader anymore and he'd retired as a minister, too. We learned about him in school during Black History Month. I never knew he had been in the army, though.

"He still helps out over at Bethel Baptist Church," Uncle Dex said. "And he comes in here every now and then. He's pretty interested in history, too."

"Do you think he would want to talk to us?" I asked. "I mean about the war?"

Uncle Dex shrugged. "He's very nice, and I'm sure if he didn't want to talk about it, he would politely let you know.

But you should drop by the church and see. He's usually there. It's over near the river, not far from here."

The river he was talking about was the Rappahannock River. The Kitchen Sink and the two main streets of downtown Fredericksburg were just a couple of blocks away.

"Maybe tomorrow," I said, not so sure about just walking up to Reverend Simpson out of the blue and asking him about the war. "I better get home for dinner. It's getting pretty late."

"Watch out for rubber chickens," Uncle Dex said.

He was just kidding around, but the whole way home on my bike — especially going past the Masonic cemetery — I kept looking around nervously for signs of Belman and his friends and their potato cannon.

CHAPTER 14

I made Greg and Julie go with me the next day, of course. I'd seen Reverend Simpson before — he spoke one time at an assembly when we were in elementary school, and in a small town like ours you're bound to run into just about everybody once in a while — but I'd never actually talked to him. Plus, I'm not too good at talking to old people, even though it seems like we've been doing a lot of that sort of thing since meeting our first ghost and solving the first mystery.

When we got to the Bethel Baptist Church, we knocked on the front door. No one came to answer, but Julie discovered the door was open, so we let ourselves in.

Inside we ran into a woman who must have been cleaning the sanctuary to get it ready for that weekend's service. "Can I help you children?" she asked. "I'm Mrs. Turner, the church secretary." She was older, too, but not super old like Reverend Simpson was the last time I saw him. "Are you lost?"

"Oh no," Julie said. "Sorry to interrupt. We're here to see Reverend Simpson."

Mrs. Turner studied us for a minute. "Is he expecting you?"

"No, ma'am," I said. "My uncle knows him, and he said we should come over and introduce ourselves to the reverend. We wanted to ask him some questions."

"Is this about civil rights?" Mrs. Turner asked. "He gets a lot of folks wanting to ask him about that time."

"Not exactly," I said. "It's actually about World War II. My uncle said Reverend Simpson was in the war."

"In North Africa," Greg added.

"Huh," Mrs. Turner said. "Well, I don't know him to speak much on that subject. Not in a very long time. And even then I know he wasn't comfortable. I believe it upsets him to remember what happened back then."

"Oh, we won't ask him to talk about anything that he'd rather not discuss," Julie assured her. It was clear to all of us that we were going to have to get past Mrs. Turner to get to Reverend Simpson, so I was glad Julie was making the case. "It's just for a history project we're working on. And we need as many primary sources as we can find. Having Reverend Simpson would be a great help because he's such an authority on so many things."

It apparently worked because Mrs. Turner carefully placed her cleaning supplies on a pew and motioned for us to follow her. "Just don't make much noise," she said. "In case he's praying. Or taking a nap." She smiled a little when she said that last part.

•   •   •

Reverend Simpson *was* taking a nap. Or that's what it looked like, anyway, when Mrs. Turner led us back down a dark hallway behind the sanctuary to a small office that might have once been a big storage closet. Reverend Simpson was sitting in a chair next to a floor lamp, his eyes closed and head drooping forward. He had an open Bible in his lap that was threatening to slide off onto the floor. Mrs. Turner rescued it and quietly placed it on a tiny table. The only other thing on the table was a glass of water.

She pressed a finger over her lips and started to lead us

away, but Reverend Simpson must have heard us because he sat up suddenly and opened his eyes.

"Someone is lost," he said. I thought at first he was looking at me and Greg and Julie and Mrs. Turner, but the way he was staring, I realized he was looking past us.

I turned, thinking there must be somebody else there — maybe even John Wollman — but it was just the empty hallway.

"It's some children, Reverend," Mrs. Turner said gently, stepping back inside the office and touching his shoulder. "They're here to speak with you if you're up for having visitors."

Reverend Simpson kept staring past us for another minute. He squinted, then shook his head and looked directly at us. He smiled. "So sorry," he said. "I thought there was someone else."

"Just us," Greg said.

Reverend Simpson considered Greg for a minute, then extended his hand, which trembled slightly, but enough to notice. Greg shook his hand. Next Reverend Simpson shook Julie's hand, and then mine, nodding his head the whole time. His hair was white and thin, and he had a long, sad face, though the sadness that I saw there disappeared when-ever he smiled. I could tell he was very tall, even folded up into the chair the way he was. He moved very slowly the whole time.

Mrs. Turner set up three folding chairs, squeezed inside the office so when we sat our knees were practically knock-ing into Reverend Simpson's. He didn't seem to mind.

"What can I do for you?" he asked once we were all settled.

"My uncle, Dex Carter, he has that antique store down-town, the Kitchen Sink," I started. "He said we should come talk to you."

Reverend Simpson nodded some more. "I do know your uncle," he said. "I knew your grandfather much better, of course. We were good friends over the years."

Pop Pop — Uncle Dex and my mom's dad — died two years ago and I still miss him a lot. I liked it that Reverend Simpson knew him and said that about him.

Reverend Simpson brought his shaky hands together under his chin. "And now what's the subject for the conver-sation you young people brought with you today?"

"Well, we wanted to ask you about your experiences in World War II," I said. "Uncle Dex said you were in the army, and you fought in the war in North Africa, and that's what we're the most interested in."

Reverend Simpson chuckled. "I'm afraid your uncle wasn't entirely correct. I did serve during the war, but I didn't fight in North Africa. None of us did."

I was confused, and from the looks on their faces, Greg and Julie were, too.

"Uh, *us*?" I hesitated. "I mean, when you say 'us,' you mean, um . . ."

He chuckled again. "Back then the word was Negroes," he said. "Or colored. Now it's African American or black. Any word you use, though, it was all the same back then. At the start of the war — for most of the war — they wouldn't let us Negro soldiers fight. They decided we weren't good enough for it. Not disciplined enough. Couldn't follow orders. Not brave enough. Not intelligent enough."

The way he said those things, I thought Reverend Simpson might spit out something sour he'd just taken a bite of.

"But that was just wrong," Greg exclaimed. "Totally ridiculous."

Julie and I nodded in agreement.

"It was different times," Reverend Simpson continued. "But that's what they thought — the government, Congress, the generals. So we weren't allowed. So yes, I was in North Africa for the entire campaign. Many of us were. Six long months in the desert and the mountains. But we mostly stayed in the rear. Drove trucks. Worked as mechanics, cooks, laborers. I even drove an ambulance for a time, which was as close as I was to the actual fighting. But they wouldn't issue us weapons, and they wouldn't let us fight. Not until much later in the war. And then there was fight enough for everybody, of every color, and they realized they needed every able-bodied man there was."

Reverend Simpson looked down at his hands, still drawn together as if he was going to pray. "We were in France and Belgium by then. Pressing hard toward Germany. I was in the 761st Tank Battalion. They called us the Black Panthers. I was part of an all-black tank crew in an all-black company in an all-black battalion. And wondering every day, as we inflicted and suffered more and more and more casualties, why it was we'd been so eager to get let into the fight."

"They should have known that all along, though," Greg said. "That the black soldiers could fight just as well as anybody. My dad said it wasn't that way in Vietnam. He said everybody fought together, white and black and Hispanic."

"The world does change, son," Reverend Simpson said. "But sometimes it seems to take a lot longer than it should. And at the time, in North Africa, the generals, they didn't want much to do with the black soldiers. Didn't mind if we cleaned their latrines, slopped their chow, changed oil, greased axles, unloaded ships, carried off those who died. But that was the long and the short of it.

"Black Americans like myself called the war the Double V Campaign. The first *V* was for the victory we all wanted over the Germans and the Japanese and the Italians, of course."

"What was the second *V*?" Julie asked.

"Victory for civil rights," Reverend Simpson answered. "We figured we'd prove ourselves in the war, and when they saw how we served and sacrificed the same as every other American, they would be hard-pressed not to change the laws back home — for equal rights to vote, to own a home and live anywhere we wanted, to ride the same public transportation, to go to decent schools with everybody else."

"Did that happen?" Greg asked. "I mean, I know there were the civil rights laws they passed, but didn't those come a lot later?"

Reverend Simpson nodded. "It took them another twenty years after the war, it's true. And there was a whole lot of struggle, which I hope you are learning all about in school. But eventually they came around."

"The Double V Campaign," Greg said. "Wow. I never heard of that."

Reverend Simpson held up both hands and made victory signs with each. Or maybe he meant for them to be peace signs since there's no difference between the two.

CHAPTER 15

"Lot of people, when you say North Africa, they think it's all desert up there," Reverend Simpson continued. "And there's plenty of desert, and there was plenty of fighting that went on in the desert. Most of the sandy desert, from what I understood at the time, was over in Egypt and Libya, where you have the sand dunes and the oil fields and the pyramids and such. But the Americans weren't over there. That all was between the Germans and the British. They had the India Army fighting over there against the Germans, too, but you don't hear much about that."

"And the Italians and the Australians," Julie added. "The Italians were with the Germans, and the Australians were with . . ." She trailed off — not because she didn't know the Australians were on our side, but because she'd interrupted Reverend Simpson. "I'm sorry, sir. I didn't mean to interrupt."

He laughed. "No need for that," he said, waving his hand. "You were right to correct me there. I had forgotten about the both of them."

Reverend Simpson shook his head, as if trying to clear some things up. "Where was I? Oh, yes. The desert. Well, like I said, the sand desert was over in those countries mostly. Where we were — the Americans, but we were fighting right alongside the English folks and the French fellows — was a rougher kind of terrain. Had your desert there, too, plus your mountains, your high ridges, your hills that just looked to grow straight up out of the ground. Seemed like the Germans had control of every one of them and we had to fight our way to the top of one after another. Except when they stopped us, which was plenty of times. And even if we took one of those hills, no telling if the Germans would hit us in a surprise attack and take it right back."

"Why?" Greg asked. "Why not just surround them on their hills, or go around them?"

"That would have been one way to do it," Reverend Simpson said. "Only if the Germans had artillery on those hills — and they usually did — they could just take aim and wipe us out as we passed. And that did happen, too, I'm sad to say. Too many times to count. We lost nearly as many men going up those slopes, too. And then sometimes they just all-out ambushed us when we were crossing flat land in their valleys. This was all in Tunisia I'm talking about, by the way. The smallest country up there in North Africa, but big enough to hold most of the Africa war. And they got graveyards there that still hold most of our men who didn't survive it."

Reverend Simpson had begun speaking in a more halting sort of way. Every now and then, he paused, taking a deep breath. I wondered if it was getting harder for him to talk about this part of the war. Probably it was.

"We read that you had to fight the French first," Julie said.

Reverend Simpson nodded. "That was a terrible surprise, and a big disappointment. Never understood what they were thinking, getting in with the Germans like they did. But thank goodness they came around quick. Wasn't quick enough for all of our boys. I didn't see it. We were back on board the transport ships when they sent in the battleships to the harbors, and the landing boats to the beaches. By the time they set us truck drivers down on shore — I was in Algeria, but there were others back in Morocco — the French had already turned around and joined our side, the Allies."

"The Germans and the Italians were the Axis, right?" Greg asked.

"Them plus the Japanese," Reverend Simpson said. "Not that the Japanese were in North Africa, of course, although they did invade China. And we were going after them all over the Pacific."

"We studied a lot about that," Greg said. "The war in the Pacific. Especially the Battle of Midway."

"That was the big one," Reverend Simpson said. He paused for a moment and took a few breaths before continuing. "Ours was big, too — all of the Tunisian campaign. Wasn't just one battle. Seemed like it was a bunch of different battles going on just about all the time once we got there and the fighting started. We had to cross Algeria, and many had to travel even farther, all the way from Morocco on the

Atlantic Coast, and get all our men and supplies and trucks and tanks and artillery landed and hauled a thousand miles before we saw the first German panzer tank. They knew we were coming, all right. And they had their reinforcements and they were all dug in by the time we made it to Tunisia."

"How scared were you?" I asked. "I mean not just you personally, but all the troops?"

"Plenty," he said. "And not nearly enough. It was supposed to be what they used to call a cakewalk. We figured to be in their biggest ports, Tunis and Bizerte, a week after we landed in November '42. Should have known better. Shouldn't ever have underestimated the Germans like we did." Reverend Simpson shook his head sadly. "So many, so many," he said.

"So many?" Julie asked, though I was pretty sure I knew what he was talking about — the men who died. And I was right.

"So many boys," Reverend Simpson said. "I still pray for them. Every single day. That they were right with the Lord when they were taken so young. You think you're going to live forever when you're young like we were, of course. You think you have all the time in the world to get things straight in your life, get things straight in your soul."

He didn't say anything else for a while, and we all just sat there in silence. I wondered if this was how it was in Quaker meetings — everybody just sitting together, praying or whatever, mulling everything over. I guessed for Reverend Simpson — and for most soldiers and anybody who'd ever been in war — it was hard to talk about with those who hadn't been there, who just knew about it from books and movies. Any sense you might start out with that war was some great adventure, heroes and bad guys and good versus evil and our side always wins — that probably vanished pretty quickly, giving way to the deep grief and maybe even despair about the horrors of war.

"They had a name for it," Reverend Simpson said, rousing himself. "That North Africa campaign. They called it Operation TORCH. I guess because we were supposed to be carrying the torch of liberty and freedom and all that. And I suppose we were. But it didn't always feel like it."

.   .   .

We sat with Reverend Simpson for another hour while he told us about the long trip they made across Algeria, before they even got to the fight with the Germans and Italians. That cakewalk he'd mentioned before. How they split up the armies — ours and the British and the French, who were supposed to be working together — and tried to capture Tunis, the capital, not even a whole week after the landing. And how bad it went. "We got our butts handed to us" was how Reverend Simpson put it. "But we didn't quit. Though from the way I heard it, we kept making the same mistakes over and over for about the next six weeks."

He shook his head. "Bloody, costly, terrible mistakes." He talked about places we'd never heard of but that apparently were really important battles during those six weeks. Tebourba was one. And Medjez-el-Bab. And Longstop Hill.

Our guys kept running up against their tanks because our tanks were no match for theirs and pretty quickly got knocked out of action. Reverend Simpson described how it was for him — a truck driver but also a mechanic — trying to repair vehicles by taking parts off other vehicles that had been mostly destroyed by the German tanks, and also by the German Stukas — their attack planes that kept strafing our troops with deadly accuracy because there were so few places to try to hide in the hard terrain.

He talked about other stuff, too, of course — not just the war. Like about taking baths in their helmets. Giving whisky to pet lizards to watch them stagger around. Betting on scorpion fights. Bartering with the local Algerians for, well, just about everything. Mostly food. How bad the villages smelled because, as the troops found out, the Algerians used human poop for fertilizer. But that didn't stop the soldiers from swiping oranges from the orange groves, and helping themselves to anything else they could find. "Guess it wasn't fair to the people that lived there," Reverend Simpson said. "But at the time you just didn't think about them. They were just a part of the landscape. And since they didn't have anything to do with the fight, we mostly ignored them when they complained about us.

"So that's how it went for the first six weeks," he concluded. "We'd take a village, the Germans would take it right back. We'd attack their hill, they'd attack our hill. We'd move forward a couple of miles, they'd push us back even farther than we'd been before. We had our own generals, of course, but Eisenhower put one of the British generals in charge of the Tunisian campaign. I guess it was a political thing, since the British had been fighting a lot longer than we had. Anyway, it was a General Kenneth Anderson in charge of North Africa and Tunisia, and our generals had to take orders from him. And lots of folks didn't like that one bit."

"How come?" Greg asked. We'd been so silent, sitting and listening to Reverend Simpson, that I'd almost forgotten he and Julie were there.

"Well, our boys thought the British were a little too uppity. Too snooty. You know. That they looked down their noses at us, like we weren't as good as them. Meanwhile, they thought the Yanks — that's what they called us Americans — didn't know what the heck we were doing. That we hadn't been trained enough, or trained right, or whatever. That we wouldn't stand and fight in battle. That sort of thing."

"What about the French?" Julie asked.

Reverend Simpson laughed. "We were all pretty much in agreement that they were, well, not exactly cowardly, but let's just say never the first to volunteer to lead the way into battle. And they were even snootier than the Brits. Of course I have to give those Brits the credit. Most of them did know how to fight. And they should, seeing as how they'd already been fighting the Germans and Italians for the past two years. So yeah, we were green and all that, but even from where I was, in the rear patching up trucks and tanks and half-tracks, I could still tell that those Brits knew what they were doing, even if they weren't a match for the Germans, either. At least not right away."

"So how did things end up?" I asked, wondering if John Wollman was around to hear all of this.

Reverend Simpson stifled a yawn. I could see we'd tired him out. "Fall turned into winter," he said. "And not a one of us was ready for that."

CHAPTER 16

Though we could tell Reverend Simpson needed a break, we seemed to have barely scratched the surface of everything he knew, and had experienced, in the war in North Africa. And there was one more thing I wanted to ask him about.

"When you were in the war, in North Africa," I started. "I know you said they wouldn't let African American soldiers fight, but were things, um, better? I mean, since everybody was there fighting for the same cause, in the same war, on the same side and everything . . ."

I trailed off. But Reverend Simpson knew what I was getting at.

"Better in some ways," he said. "By that I mean that since white soldiers were under orders not to be racist, say racist things, to black soldiers, then there was a whole lot less of that sort of thing than many of us were used to. But that doesn't mean it didn't still happen, of course. And that also doesn't mean that black fellows didn't stand up to that business a little more once they were in uniform. I still got called the same names you all likely still hear sometimes today. And I have to admit I got into a few scrapes over it myself. But there were a lot of officers who just saw us as soldiers with a job to do, and that was the end of it. Some of them even said to us that they thought we ought to be let into the actual fighting, that they knew we had it in us to be just as brave and just as strong and just as good on the front lines as any white soldier.

"But it was still mostly segregated. Where we set up our tents and where they set up theirs. Where we ate and where they ate. Where we got treated by the medics and where they got treated by the field surgeons. Where we got crammed into the transport ships and where they got to stay. The kinds of jobs we did and the kinds of jobs they did. Couldn't keep us entirely apart, of course. It was a war, after all. But there was still plenty of segregated America that shipped out those boats over to Africa."

· · ·

We ended things there, though Reverend Simpson invited us to come back and visit with him again soon, and he said he'd be happy to answer more of our questions about the war, as long as he had the energy to. I looked back as we walked away from him down the hall from his little office. His head was already drooped forward, chin to his chest, and I could hear him softly snoring.

As soon as we got outside on the sidewalk, Greg asked the question that had been in the back of all our minds since we first showed up to visit Reverend Simpson.

"Did you see the way he looked right past us when we first came in?"

"Yes!" exclaimed Julie. "And he said it looked like someone was lost!"

"So you guys think maybe he saw John Wollman? That John was there with us?"

"Maybe," Greg said. "Only Reverend Simpson didn't say anything about it if he did. And except for that one second, he didn't look past us at anybody, or anything, the whole rest of the time we were there."

"I had a feeling that John was close by," I said. "At least I think I did. But maybe I just hoped he was so he could hear everything Reverend Simpson was saying about North Africa."

"Wishful thinking," Julie said. "I know what you mean. I was hoping the same thing."

"If he shows up tonight at your house, you should call us," Greg said. "Even if he wasn't here listening to Reverend Simpson we can always fill him in on what he missed."

"Yeah, but it seems to be better if a ghost hears that stuff for himself," I said. "At least based on what's happened with our first two ghosts."

Julie nodded and said, "We'll see."

We still had a little time before we all had to be home, so we stopped off at the Kitchen Sink for a short band practice. I noticed something as we were all tuning our instruments, and as Julie was warming up on the keyboard: We were all humming that "Simple Gifts" song!

"Hey, where did you guys hear that?" I asked.

They were oblivious, though. "Hear what?" Greg asked.

"Yes," said Julie. "Hear what?"

"'Simple Gifts,'" I said. "That song you were just humming."

They looked at each other and both shrugged. They still didn't know what I was talking about, so I let it go. We did a quick run-through of Julie's hamster and antibullying songs, our standards, as she called them. Julie said she was still working on her rap song, but she wasn't ready to play it for us yet, or teach it to us.

"We're just that one perfect song away," Greg said, sounding uncharacteristically optimistic. "I can feel it."

"No way," I said. "Even if Julie writes the best rap ever, Belman and the Bass Rats are too good. They're eighth graders. They kill us every time."

"Oh, by the way," Julie said, "I thought I would tell you guys, just in case you're interested, not that you probably are, and not that you would probably want to come anyway, but, you know, just in case, um . . ."

"What?" I asked impatiently. I couldn't believe it was taking her so long to say whatever it was she was trying — and failing — to get out. This wasn't like Julie at all.

"Yeah, what?" Greg asked, his voice a lot softer than mine. And, I guess, nicer.

Julie gave me a dirty look. She smiled at Greg. "Okay, well, here it is. I have a piano recital. Friday night. And you're invited." She shifted her gaze to me. "Both of you."

"A recital?" I repeated. "Like Beethoven and Mozart and stuff like that?"

"I didn't know you took piano lessons," Greg added.

Julie sighed. Then she played the opening bars of a really pretty classical song that even I could recognize called "Für Elise." And sure enough, it was by old Beethoven.

"Wow," said Greg. "Of *course* we'll be there. What are we supposed to wear?"

"Just regular clothes," Julie said. "You know, nice pants, nice shoes, nice shirt."

"Will there be food?" Greg asked. "I mean, it's okay if there's not. I was just wondering."

"Oh sure," Julie said. "Finger sandwiches, petit fours. That sort of thing."

"I don't know what those are," Greg said, "but sounds good to me."

Julie just laughed.

•　　•　　•

Since we didn't know if or when Belman and his friends might try to attack us again with their potato cannon, Greg and I rode our bikes all the way to Julie's house with her. "You really don't have to do this," she said, but we could tell she liked it — us being her escorts or guardians or whatever.

Greg and I rode together over to our own houses after we dropped her off. "I feel bad about that money," I said.

"What money?" Greg asked.

"The money Julie said she was going to send the guy for John Wollman's letters," I said. "She didn't even ask us to contribute or anything. She just said she'd take care of it."

Greg shrugged. "She probably has more money than us. She can afford it."

"I doubt it," I said. "We were just in her neighborhood. It's kind of run-down. And her house is smaller than my house."

"I guess you're right," Greg said.

"So we should give her some money," I said. "At least pay our fair share."

"But how?" he asked. "I probably have about two dollars to my name. Maybe two fifty if I look under the couch cushions and stuff like that."

"Same for me," I said. "Which is why we have to win the open mic competition. I heard they pay you fifty dollars if you win, which is how much that guy is charging for the letters."

"I don't know," he said. "That's going to be pretty hard, don't you think?"

"Well, what else can we do?"

Greg didn't answer, but I thought about it for a couple of minutes as we rode the rest of the way to Greg's. I kept thinking about it as we sat on our bikes in his driveway, until his dad came out and yelled for Greg to come inside for dinner. He even invited me to stay and eat dinner with them, which I was pretty sure he'd never done before.

I wished I could, but I knew Mom was expecting me home. "Thanks anyway, Mr. Troutman," I said.

"Well, I better go," I said to Greg as I started to pedal away. And then I stopped so suddenly I nearly crashed my bike.

"I've got it!" I said.

"What?" he asked.

"We'll be buskers."

"Uh, yeah, sure," Greg said, pulling off his beanie and scratching his head. "And what's a busker?"

I was already back on my bike. "It's a street performer," I said. "We'll set up on a corner downtown and play our guitars. People will stop and listen and throw dollars in our guitar cases. I bet we'll make a ton of money!"

CHAPTER 17

I knew about busking from Uncle Dex, who told me he saw a lot of people doing it when he traveled in Europe after graduating from college. He tried it with his ukulele when he was in Spain and said he actually made enough to buy dinner. I figured what worked there would probably work even better in Fredericksburg, though when I told Mom and Dad about the plan they burst out laughing again.

"What's so funny?" I demanded.

"Nothing, nothing, sweetheart," Mom said. We had just sat down to dinner.

She and Dad exchanged a smile. "You just sounded so

grown-up using that word," Mom said. "I think it sounds like a great idea. You've always been so shy. It's good that you're willing to try new things."

"What got you so interested in street performing all of a sudden?" Dad asked.

I hesitated, and then told them about Julie and John Wollman III and the letters. I once again left out the part about John Wollman being a ghost, of course. Mom and Dad knew Julie, Greg, and I were really big into solving war mysteries. They just didn't know why exactly.

"Fifty dollars! That's a lot of money," Dad said. "Did she have permission from her parents?"

"Oh yeah," I said. "Her mom even negotiated with the guy to get us a better deal."

"I hope the letters turn out to be worth it," Dad said. "Is this something else you're researching for school — another history project?"

"Sort of," I said. I hated lying to Mom and Dad, so I didn't want to just say yes.

"Well, enough about that for now. Everybody eat up," Mom said. "But, Anderson, you'll have to tell us all about the letters once you get them. And your dad and I want you to let us know, too, before you go contacting strangers about anything like this, even if it's for a good cause."

• • •

I was dead asleep when John Wollman came that night. He might have been sitting there for hours, not wanting to wake me. He might have just shown up. All I knew was that I sat up suddenly in my bed and there he was, sitting in my desk chair again. His head was bowed, his eyes closed, his chin on his fists. He might have been praying, though he didn't say if he was or not. He just opened his eyes when I sat up. Then he smiled and nodded and said, "Hi, Anderson."

I said, "Hi, John," as if it was the most natural thing in the world, and I guess it was becoming kind of a normal thing for ghosts to keep showing up in my bedroom like that.

My mind was totally clear, somehow, instead of foggy from sleep. "Were you there this afternoon?" I asked. "At Reverend Simpson's office? He acted almost as if he saw you with us, or behind us, or something."

John shook his head. "Afraid not. At least I don't think so. It's been hard to bring things into focus since the last time I was here. Or wherever I was when I last saw you. Seems like everything's getting harder. I can't exactly explain it. So it's possible I was there, but it's also possible that I wasn't, if that makes sense." He laughed softly.

"I guess that all must sound pretty weird," he admitted. "Well, never mind. Who's Reverend Simpson and what did I miss?"

I explained as quickly as I could about who Reverend Simpson was, and about him being in North Africa, too, and about the African American soldiers and the Double V Campaign. Then I racked my brain to remember the names of all the battles in Tunisia that Reverend Simpson had told us about.

John kept nodding. "Those do sound familiar," he said when I finished, meaning the names of the battles. "And the African American soldiers — is that what you called them? — that's the same as the Negro troops, I'm guessing. That's the word they used back then, though some used worse terms, unfortunately."

"Yeah," I said. "We use different terms now for a lot of things."

"We had a standing order about who we were supposed to treat," John said. "I do remember that. If it was a choice between a wounded German or a wounded American or Brit, we treated the American or the Brit first. And our commanding officer also told us medics that if it was a choice between treating a white soldier or a Negro, we were supposed to treat the white soldier. They said it was because white soldiers on our side were the ones in combat and we needed them the most But if it was a German or Italian, then we could treat the Negro soldier first."

"So what did you do?" I asked. "Do you remember?"

"I guess I just went on ahead and treated everybody I could," John said. "They were all God's children. At least that's what they taught us at the Friends meetings my whole life growing up."

"Were there very many?" I asked.

"Very many who?" John responded. "White soldiers, German soldiers, Negro soldiers?"

"I guess all of them."

John studied his hands as if he might start counting on his fingers. "I can't really say. Every day just seemed like more and more and more of the same. You mentioned those places: Tebourba and Longstop Hill. I kind of remember those, like I said, but what I can picture is the bodies. Some of them still alive. A lot already gone. I remember running from one to another, and another after that. Trying to stop their bleeding. Carrying them off the battlefield when we could — which wasn't all the time, because plenty of times the Germans had us medics pinned down, too. Or those German Stukas attacking from the air and we were hugging the ground like everybody else, praying we wouldn't get hit. And I remember any time we saw those big tanks of theirs coming at us, everybody wanted to turn and run. Those were the Tigers, the new ones that the Germans started sending into the field. Shells from our little Sherman tanks couldn't penetrate their front armor from point-blank range, but they could knock out one of ours from a mile away."

He paused and shook his head, remembering. "I guess a lot of it's coming back to me after all, but it's like those newsreels we used to see at the movie theaters back home, before I went to the war. Lots of bombs and explosions and shooting and men running around and torn up flags still waving, but you couldn't tell what exactly was going on if it wasn't for the announcer telling you. And when you're in the real war, in the real battles in those places you said in Tunisia, there's no announcer except your officers yelling at you all the time." He paused again. "And those poor soldiers yelling, too, only not giving you orders, just yelling, and screaming, and begging for help. The only worse sound than that was when they went quiet. Then you knew they were beyond any help you could ever give."

I hated how quickly my conversations with John turned so dark like this, and I had to think he hated it, too. Not talking to me about stuff. He seemed to like that. But the way we always ended up talking about all the casualties, which made sense, of course, since John had been a medic and it was his job to try to save them. Plus, I knew we had to keep exploring that stuff, and everything else we could, until we discovered what happened to him in the war, and how he ended up AWOL, and how he died.

I decided we should take a break from talking about all that, though, and told John about my plan with Greg to do music downtown and make a bunch of money.

He laughed, though not as hard as Mom and Dad, and not in quite the same way. "I'd love to see something like that," he said, not seeming to mind me changing the subject at all. "They used to have a lot of that sort of thing when I was a boy. I remember me and my brother, we had jobs running to the Italian Market over on Ninth Street for people in our building where we lived in Philadelphia. Older folks, women with too many little kids, anybody too busy. We got to keep whatever change there was, usually. But we always gave some to guys playing accordion with their dancing monkey, or jugglers juggling fruit — especially if they dropped a melon and it split open on the ground. Then we got free eats."

·   ·   ·

John talked about growing up in Philadelphia for a little while, mostly about his younger brother, Aaron. Aaron had polio when he was little, and one leg was shorter than the other as a result, which was another reason John thought he probably wasn't ever drafted into the army. "He had to stay home and take care of Mother, too," John added. "We'd already lost Father by that time, and Mother never really got over it. So somebody had to be there with her."

"He must have really loved you," I said. "To name his own son John Wollman Jr."

"Yeah," John said. "He did love me, and I loved him. He even said it to me sometimes — that he loved me. Not something a lot of guys in our old neighborhood would be caught dead saying to their brother or their friend or anybody. He was always so close to Mother. It's a blessing that he actually met somebody and married her and had a family of his own.

I was glad to learn about that. And that he had a boy of his own, too."

"Hopefully we'll get your old letters home from the war tomorrow, or sometime this week," I said. "Then we'll get to learn more about you, too."

CHAPTER 18

I went to the library the next day at school during study hall to read more about the war in North Africa and the Tunisian campaign. We'd already learned a lot, but it still felt disjointed — bits and pieces of a war, like John said.

What I read helped pull those pieces together a little better. There was the invasion, of course — an armada of our ships crossing the Atlantic Ocean from Norfolk, Virginia, which was just a few hours from Fredericksburg. And they did it in secret, which was a pretty amazing thing. The Germans were busy fighting the Soviet Union by that time, since they had already dominated the rest of Europe (except for England, of course). They were supposed to have what they called a nonaggression pact with Joseph Stalin, the Soviet leader, so neither would attack the other, and so the Soviet Union wouldn't take the side of the Allies. No big surprise, though, that Hitler broke the pact and decided to try to take over the Soviet Union. But it ended badly for Hitler and Germany, because they had to send so many troops and weapons and equipment and supplies and planes there — and they still couldn't defeat the Soviet Union. On top of that, they ended up with millions killed in the fighting on what they called the Eastern Front.

But even with the Germans bogged down fighting the Soviets, the Americans and British got bogged down fighting the Germans in North Africa. So what was supposed to just take a month turned into a whole long frozen winter of waiting to attack them again in Tunisia. That was where Reverend Simpson had left off telling us his story.

It wasn't until February 1943, three months after the U.S. landed in North Africa, that the Allies launched another offensive, but instead of us sweeping the Germans and Italians out of Tunisia, things got even worse for us. At first it looked like the surprise attack might finally mean some movement deeper into Tunisia, but then it turned into a major counterattack with the Germans chasing us almost all the way back into Algeria at a place called the Kasserine Pass. That was the place where the Americans and British and French forces had to retreat into the mountains as the Germans — with their better tanks and better-trained army and better tactics and better just about everything — threatened to end the invasion altogether, and destroy our airfields and supply dumps, and force us all the way back, maybe even to Morocco.

I got really depressed reading about all of this — and reading again and again about how unprepared we were for war with the Germans, who'd been fighting all over Europe for three or four years by then, with nobody able to stop them, except the British, sort of.

And every time I read about another battle, and more of our soldiers getting wounded or dying, I thought about John Wollman with his medic's kit, running from one man to the next, tying tourniquets, pouring sulfa powder over wounds, pressing on gauze, giving morphine injections, yelling for litter bearers to carry another casualty — another American, another Brit, another Frenchman — to ambulances sometimes hidden far from the fighting, and surgeons' tents even farther in the rear. Too far for many of the casualties.

And John and the other medics were doing this with bullets and bombs going off all around them, and with German Stukas shooting from above while the German tanks rolled across the battlefield.

The Kasserine Pass. That name got stuck in my head and for the rest of the day it stayed there, like a song you can't stop from playing over and over in your mind, even if you don't particularly like it. It was the biggest battle in the whole war in North Africa, and it was where we got our butts kicked the worst and ended up running from the enemy in a full-on retreat.

But right after the Kasserine Pass disaster in February 1943, they brought in General Patton to lead our army and somehow or another everything turned around and we actually started winning. One thing I read said that the Germans had made a huge mistake fighting the Soviets and us at the same time. They didn't have enough troops to defeat both enemies. Plus, they were horribly unprepared for the bitter cold Soviet winter. Which meant that in North Africa, after the Kasserine Pass, the Germans couldn't hold the Allies off. The Allies were finally able to defeat the Germans and Italians and force them to retreat back into Tunisia.

Unfortunately, that wasn't the end of it, though. There were more battles through March and April 1943 — a lot more battles, at places whose names I had never heard of and could barely pronounce, like Mareth, and El Guettar, and Maknassy Pass, and Fondouk Pass. But finally, in May that year, we won, forcing the Germans and Italians all the way back to the two major port cities of Bizerte and Tunis. We bombed Bizerte so bad that there was literally nobody left alive there, and not a single building left standing. I was glad we beat the bad guys, but I still felt kind of awful when I read that.

Since we now controlled those two cities, our planes were able to bomb any ship trying to cross the Mediterranean to bring fresh troops or weapons or supplies over from Italy, or to ferry Germans or Italians trying to escape from Tunisia. And that was the end of the war in North Africa, except for the problem of what to do with three hundred thousand German and Italian prisoners of war.

There were seventy thousand Allied casualties — nearly twenty thousand of them Americans — but that chapter of World War II was finally over.

Only we still didn't know what happened to John Wollman.

We got our answer — part of it, at least — that afternoon when Julie burst into our practice room at the Kitchen Sink, waving a large envelope.

"I got them!" she exclaimed. "Finally!"

"The letters?" Greg asked, as if it wasn't totally obvious.

Julie opened the envelope to show us, jumping up and down with excitement.

I was disappointed, though, because all she pulled out were a few pieces of really old paper so thin they could have passed for tissues.

"Uh, how many are there?" I asked.

"I don't know," she said, now looking a little disappointed herself. "Just a few." She counted them and then revised her figure. "Six. But some of whatever was written has been blacked out."

She held one of the letters up to the light, then shook her head. "Still can't see what's blacked out."

"Well, let's just read them," Greg suggested. "There might be something important."

Julie looked around the room. "John's not here?"

"Haven't seen him," Greg said. "Anderson talked to him last night. He said he remembered some of those battles that

Reverend Simpson told us about, but he said mostly it was all this giant blur of running from one soldier to the next, trying to save them."

"He still couldn't say what happened to him," I added. "We talked some about him growing up in Philadelphia, though. He remembered some stuff about that. He remembered his brother and where he lived and his parents and everything."

Julie laid the envelope down on her keyboard and selected one of the letters. "This one is the first he wrote," she said. Then she started reading.

"Dear Mother and Aaron, Thank you for your letters. All the guys here read their letters to one another because we all miss home and it's nice to hear about home, even if it's not your home. I can't tell you where I am right now and even if I did the censors would black out what I wrote, plus I would lose mail privileges and I don't want that to happen. But we're on the move and up to something big, although they haven't told us what yet. At least with something to speculate about nobody's been giving me a hard time about being a conscientious objector, so that's one thing

for me to be grateful for. The food is terrible as usual.
It's hard to keep anything down, though, so I guess it
doesn't matter. I hope you are both keeping warm and
staying well and in God's embrace. All my love, John."

We were all so intent on listening to her read that we didn't even notice that John had joined us until she finished.

He spoke first. "I wrote that on the troop ship, crossing the Atlantic," he said. "I remember. By the time they received the letter, we had already crossed, and the invasion had started, and we were deep into it in Tunisia. It was the dead of winter and I was treating a lot of frostbite."

CHAPTER 19

"Should I read another one?"
Julie asked. "Or do you want to read them yourself
first?"

She offered the letters to John. He started to reach for
them, but then stopped.

"No," he said. "You go ahead. Please."

So Julie read the second letter, or tried to.

*"Dear Aaron, Once again I can't tell you where I am
except that it's in North Africa but besides that I'm not
allowed to say anything except . . ."*

She looked up at John. "The censors blacked out the next couple of lines, so I guess you weren't allowed to say that, either, whatever it was."

He smiled. "Who knows? Anything we said that made any reference to geography they told us they were going to delete. Anything about our positions or plans or casualty figures or the enemy's movements or tactics. Well, you get the picture."

Julie nodded, then turned her attention back to the letter.

"One thing I can tell you about is the French had some of the Algerians fighting with them, wild-looking fellows on horseback, all decked out with swords and rifles and bright costumes and feathers and such. A company of them rode down into a valley to attack German tanks, thinking they could outmaneuver anything armored. Only a squad of Stukas swooped in with their machine guns blazing. The poor Algerians didn't have a chance. By the time we got to them not a man or horse was left alive. We had to leave them there on the field. No way to get near enough to get the

men. No way to do anything for the poor horses. But enough about the war. I don't know why I even wrote about that incident. There have been so many. I should write instead about the beautiful sunsets here, especially in the desert. And about the kindness of men. Some of our medics, they've been donating pint after pint of their own blood for transfusions to soldiers who need it, even though it leaves them weak and exhausted, and even though they can't stop to rest, because if they did it might mean one more life lost on the battlefield that could have been saved."

I watched John's face as Julie read the letters and wondered if he was one of the medics who donated blood. I bet he was, though I could tell he was the kind of guy who wouldn't just come out and tell us. He was too humble for that.

He nodded thoughtfully the whole time but didn't say anything. Julie paused when she finished the second letter and we all waited to see if it would spark any memories, or anything John wanted to share with us, anyway. But he stayed quiet, so Julie picked up another and we crowded around this time, reading silently to ourselves.

Dear Aaron,

Sorry I haven't written in a while. We have a new commander, Colonel ███████████, and he doesn't seem to like me very much. The good news is he doesn't seem to like anybody very much. The bad news is he doesn't like me even more than he doesn't like anybody else, which is really saying a lot. Once he found out I was 1-A-O, he decided I needed to be on the worst details, so now I'm the body parts guy, which is about as terrible as it sounds — finding what's left of some of the casualties and putting them in body bags. Actually, it's a lot worse than it sounds. Please don't tell Mother about any of this as I know it will upset her. I'll write her a separate letter that won't mention anything about what I'm doing. Colonel ███████████ also sends me out into the worst fighting. Once to help some of our guys who were pinned down so badly that three other medics were already casualties trying to get to them. I got some shrapnel in my leg, but it was shallow and I was able to dig it out okay. Colonel ███████████ calls me Corporal Chicken ████, which would bother me more except it's not very original. I must have been called that a thousand times when I was in training.

The only thing Colonel ▮▮▮▮▮▮▮ *hates worse*
than me — and I guess the Germans and Italians —
is the Negro troops on our side. I don't understand it,
but it's how a lot of guys feel, unfortunately, and they
say things I won't repeat in this letter or in any letter.

"Wow," Julie said, interrupting the silence.

"All pretty terrible," John acknowledged.

"What is a 1-A-O?" Greg asked.

"Sort of like a conscientious objector," John said. "It means that my religion prevented me from fighting, but I was still willing to serve in the army, just not in a combat role. So I didn't have to learn how to fire a weapon. Instead I agreed to serve in the medical corps."

"Do you remember that commander you mentioned, Colonel, um, whatever?" I asked.

"Now I do," John said. "Wish I didn't, but yeah." He shook his head. "Guess there are some good things about not being too clearheaded about what happened to you in the past."

"Do you remember anything else about him besides what's in the letter?" Julie prompted.

"Just that it was a pretty constant thing, once he transferred to the medical corps battalion," John said. "Of course we were all so busy, and most of the time I was assigned to an infantry platoon, so it could be days or weeks between times I saw him — or rather he saw me. That would only be when they pulled me from the front lines, out of the platoon, and instead had me working in the rear in a field hospital. And he was busy, too. He was an officer, but he was also a surgeon, and a darn good one. But I guess what you'd call a misanthrope."

"What's that?" Greg asked.

"Someone who doesn't like people," Julie answered.

"Oh," Greg said. "I thought it was, like, somebody who was a racist, because of what you wrote about him hating the black soldiers."

" 'Judge not, that ye be not judged,' " John said. " 'For with what judgment ye judge, ye shall be judged.' "

We all stared at him for a minute.

He smiled and said, "That's according to Jesus." He smiled again. "But I guess Colonel Buncombe did seem to be that sort of person. From what I can recall. That was his name — what the censors blacked out. I can still picture him in my mind and still hear his voice — how he barked at you instead of just talking or giving regular orders. At least I can still see him and hear him from the first weeks he was there. After that, well, it all gets blurry again."

"Colonel Buncombe," Greg repeated. "That's a funny name."

"I believe it means 'nonsense,'" Julie said.

"Really, Julie?" I asked. "You even know that word?"

"We had to learn it for the spelling bee in fourth grade," she said.

"Which Julie won," Greg said to John.

"Congratulations," John said. "I never was a very good speller. And I didn't know that's what the colonel's name meant, either. Would have been a good thing to know back during the war. I bet my fellow medics would have liked to know that our new commander was named Colonel Nonsense."

And I bet John was just saying that about being a bad speller, and not knowing the definition of "buncombe," to make Greg not feel dumb.

"How about another letter?" Greg suggested.

We read two more, both of them really short, both heavily redacted, which Julie told us was what you called it when the censors blacked stuff out. They were similar to the first letter and addressed to both John's mother and his brother. Neither one said much.

The one after that was just addressed to Aaron again.

Dear Aaron,

I've really stepped into it this time. Colonel ███████ *says he's having me court-martialed. I could be kicked out of the medical corps, out of the army altogether. I could even be sent to jail. It's complicated, and I'm feeling sick to my stomach just writing this. We've got the Germans on the run now and their POWs have been pouring into our camps. I've spent more time treating them than our own troops — mostly because there are so many of them, and because our casualty rate has dropped now that we're*

███████████████████████

███████████████████████

"There's not much here," Julie said, after we finished. "About the court-martial or anything else."

"It doesn't ever say why?" I asked frantically. "What charges? What John did?"

Julie shook her head. "It just says, '*We needed so much blood for transfusions, we had to go out and beat the bushes for donors. So that's why I . . .*'"

"Then what?" Greg asked. "So that's why he what?"

"It doesn't say," Julie repeated. "Everything is redacted after that."

We all turned to John to ask him about the court-martial, but couldn't.

He was gone.

CHAPTER 20

Greg and I met up at the
Kitchen Sink the next afternoon to start our career as street
performers. He didn't like the word "busker," which I guess
is more something they say in Europe than in America anyway, so I gave it up, even though I thought it sounded cool
to say.

Uncle Dex let us plug in our amplifiers inside his store.
We had a couple of long extension cords he let us borrow
snaking outside and down the sidewalk a little ways to the
corner where we set up to play. I was so nervous I thought I
would throw up again, like I did at the last all-ages open
mic night. Greg was nervous, too, but the way he dealt with

it was by telling a lot of jokes. Really stupid ones, too: Interrupting Cow, Interrupting Ghost, Interrupting Space Alien. And stupid puns, of course. He was really big on those. "Hey, Anderson," he said as we tuned our guitars. "It was really foggy this morning. So foggy I tried to catch some."

He waited until I sighed and said, "Okay, so what happened?"

He said, "I mist," and laughed.

I groaned.

Greg opened his guitar case in front of us and we started playing — me doing rhythm guitar and Greg doing the melodies on lead guitar, though neither of us had exactly mastered our techniques quite yet. We probably didn't sound awful, but we probably didn't sound like the sort of street performers who were going to make much money.

But, boy, was I wrong. Every older person who walked by — especially the ones who looked like they could be our grandmothers — smiled and told us what a good job we were doing, and keep up the hard work. And then they carefully pulled a dollar out of their purses, making sure we could see how much, and put it in Greg's guitar case.

"If they could pat us on the head and pinch our cheeks, they'd probably want to do that, too," I said after one even told us how much we reminded her of her grandson.

"Hey, if it meant they'd throw in a little something extra, I wouldn't mind at all," Greg said.

We kept playing for an hour and a half, the same couple of songs over and over. Greg tried to get me to sing, but I was too nervous for that and told him definitely, absolutely, no. But then two old ladies stopped in front of us and listened through an entire song. I thought they would leave once we finished but they didn't. One pulled out a five-dollar bill. I practically threw down my guitar and jumped over to grab it before she changed her mind.

Only she didn't put it in Greg's case. "You boys are just the cutest things," she said.

"They sure are," said her friend.

"Now if you'll sing one of your songs, too, I'll put this in with your other dollars," the first lady said.

"It's a five-dollar bill," her friend added, as if we couldn't see.

"Sure," said Greg. "We'd be glad to. I mean Anderson would be glad to. He's our singer."

I was caught. I gave Greg a look that he knew meant I was going to kill him later, and then, as he started strumming and I joined in, I stumbled my way through a very shaky version of that hamster song of Julie's. The two old ladies laughed their butts off the whole time, but at least they left us with the five once we finished. A couple of other people walked by during the song, too, and threw in some loose change.

After the hour and a half that we were out there, cranking through our very limited repertoire, Uncle Dex finally came out of his store. "Here's ten dollars," he said. "It's yours on one condition."

"What?" I asked, reaching for the money.

"That you take the rest of the day off. You've been out here quite a while, and it's been great getting to hear you. But maybe it's time for a well-earned break. What do you say?"

Greg shrugged and I did, too. We'd raised enough to help pay for the letters, so we were done anyway.

· · ·

We had told Julie we couldn't meet to practice that afternoon, so she had no idea what we were up to. Our plan was to go to her piano recital the next night and surprise her with the money. Even though the letters hadn't turned out the way we'd hoped, because of all that redaction in them, they still had taken us closer to solving the mystery of what happened to John Wollman in the war in North Africa.

At least we hoped so. John hadn't shown up that night at my house, or at all the next day at school. And if he was anywhere nearby while we were playing on the street corner, we were probably lousy enough — and repeating ourselves so much — that he didn't stay around very long. We still had a ton of things to ask him about. I was hoping the time away would give him a chance to remember more. Julie said maybe the court-martial had something to do with the German prisoners of war. And maybe John's disappearance — his going AWOL — had something to do with it, too.

Julie's recital was at the downtown library, not too far from where Greg and I lived, so we rode our bikes over that evening, even though it was dark. We both had helmet lights so we could see in front of us and so people could see us, and Mom made me swear we would stay on the sidewalks the whole way there and back.

We were just locking our bikes up at the stand in front of the library when we heard a familiar voice behind us.

"Aren't you baby chicks out a little late on your own?" It was Belman, of course. "Shouldn't you be back at the hen-house sitting in a nest somewhere with your mother hens?"

Before we could respond, somebody did it for us. "Oh, please," said a little girl walking next to him. "Is that the best you can do?"

Belman laughed. "You're right," he said. "Must be off my game a little tonight."

The two of them blew past us, trailing a middle-aged woman who must have been their mom. They headed into the library annex, which had a small auditorium and a stage, and which was where Julie's recital was supposed to be.

"I'm betting that was Belman's sister," Greg said. "Same snarky voice."

"Yeah, probably so," I said. "Sounds as mean as him. Do you think she's in the piano recital, too?"

"I guess," Greg said. "Why else would they be here?"

"This town is way too small," I said. Greg agreed.

Julie and her parents were already there when we walked in — sitting in the front row. Julie, maybe sensing we had arrived or maybe just looking around to see if we were there, turned and saw us and gave a quick wave. Her parents turned and waved, too. An older woman in a very flowery dress was playing some very complicated song on a very big piano up on the stage. The room was filling up fast.

"There are the Belmans," Greg said, gesturing to the opposite side of the room. "And check this out." He had picked up a program from somewhere. "It's not the sister who's in the recital; it's Belman himself."

"You're kidding," I said. "Let me see that." I checked and sure enough, it was true. I guess it made sense. Belman played the keyboards in his band, the Bass Rats, but it never occurred to me that he might take lessons.

"Great," I said. "We have to hear him play before it's Julie's turn."

Greg had gotten quiet all of a sudden. He took the program, studied it for a minute, then handed it back. "Looks like about twenty minutes before he goes on."

I shrugged. "I guess so."

"I'll be back," Greg said. And before I could ask where he was going, he took off.

I was mystified but couldn't do anything about it now, so I just took a seat on Julie's side of the auditorium. She turned back and waved again, this time with a quizzical look on her face. She mouthed "Where's Greg?" but I just had to shrug again. She frowned.

The first couple of kids in the recital were terrible. The piano teacher — the same lady who had been playing when we walked in — sat next to them on the bench and practically held their hands and stabbed their little fingers for them on the keys.

And then it was Belman's turn. He was totally smirking as he walked up onstage. The piano teacher retreated — probably afraid of him and the way he was acting all super junior Beethoven. The way he sat down at the bench, you'd think he was at Carnegie Hall instead of a small-town library — though in fairness to our library, I've always thought it was one of the most awesome places around.

What was even worse than having to sit there and listen to Belman play was having to sit there and listen to him play and admit that he was really good. The title of whatever he was playing seemed to be written in German in the program, and I didn't recognize the composer. It went on for a really long time, and I wasn't sure Belman was even looking at his music, though a couple of times the piano teacher appeared back onstage to turn the page in front of him.

And then something dropped out of the sky (or out of the rafters up onstage) and landed on Belman's head. An egg. And then a second egg. Bull's-eye each time. He jumped up after the second one, wiped the yolk out of his eyes, then stared up to the rafters — just in time to see a rubber chicken also drop on his head, knocking him down, though from the way he immediately started yelling and cursing, I was pretty sure he wasn't hurt.

Embarrassed, definitely, but not hurt.

He held the rubber chicken by the throat up in front of him, as if he thought it was the chicken's fault, and not whoever was busy scrambling out of the rafters and bolting out of the library through a side door. Everybody in the audience — after gasping and a couple of them screaming — burst out laughing.

"Oh my gosh!" Belman's sister shrieked, louder than anybody. "Is that my rubber chicken?"

Julie was standing now, too, with everybody else, only instead of cracking up about what had just happened to Belman, she was turned all the way around and staring at me, her eyes wide.

I turned my hands palms up, to try to let her know I was innocent — that it was just Greg, finally getting his revenge.

CHAPTER 21

John Wollman didn't show up that night, or the next day. When Greg, Julie, and I got together for band practice Sunday afternoon, we spent as much time hoping he'd show up and speculating on what might have happened to him as we did rehearsing for the next open mic competition.

"It's got to be the court-martial," Greg said — and not for the first time. We'd been through every conceivable theory. "He got so upset hearing about that from the letters that he just doesn't have the heart to try to find out more."

"More likely it's just the energy drain," Julie said. "I've said it before — the ghosts only have a certain amount of energy to reveal themselves to us. We wasted too much of his time on trivial things when we should have been encouraging him to save himself, or save the energy of himself."

"But we never know how much energy or whatever it is a particular ghost will have," I pointed out. "They've all been so different. I just hope John will manage to come back."

"But we don't have anything else to tell him if he does," Julie said. She was more frustrated in some ways than any of us. She believed in research, and if you couldn't find the answer to something, it was because you didn't research hard enough, or deep enough, or in a disciplined enough way.

I knew — and I know — that there are some mysteries that all the research in the world can't solve — like what becomes of our ghosts once we've figured out what happened to them in their wars, and what happens to them if we don't.

I also knew it wouldn't make Julie feel any better to tell her that.

· · ·

After Friday night's piano recital incident, we were nervous about going back to school and seeing Belman. Fortunately we didn't see him over the weekend, so we hoped that maybe he would have a chance to calm down, and maybe even see the humor in what Greg did. Not that Greg was going to admit to anything. Nobody at the recital knew Greg was the one who dropped the eggs and the chicken except Julie and me, though obviously Belman must have had his suspicions. His very strong suspicions.

Oddly, Julie wasn't even mad at Greg for messing up her piano recital. She still got to play, so that might have been the main reason. And since Belman wasn't able to finish, Julie was the bright, shining star of the evening, so that must have helped her mood the next time she saw Greg, too.

Finally, though, Monday came, and so did Belman. We saw him at lunch when he marched straight across the cafeteria to confront us, knocking over a couple of other sixth graders on the way.

Greg and I ducked, ready to dive under our table and crawl out through everybody's legs, but Julie stood her ground. Literally. She jumped to her feet and held up her cell phone as if it was a sword.

"Hold it right there, Belman," she commanded, and, unbelievably, he stopped — so quickly the Three Stooges collided into him.

"Out of my way, twerp girl," Belman snarled. "I know it was that little ferret who dropped the eggs on my head."

"Wasn't there a rubber chicken, too?" Julie asked. "Don't forget that."

Belman actually growled. "I'm not going to forget anything. Now get out of my way."

Julie shook her head. She was like Joan of Arc. I couldn't believe it.

"I just have three words for you," she said, waggling her cell phone at Belman.

"Oh yeah?" he said. "What three words?"

"Potato cannon photos," Julie responded.

Belman froze. "You wouldn't," he snapped. It was an order, but Julie didn't seem to notice or care.

"Oh, don't think for a second I won't," Julie said. "If you do anything to Greg or Anderson, the evidence goes straight to the police. And to your mom." She smiled and then added, "We might even tell your little sister."

Belman growled again. I thought his head would explode. Then he spun on his heels and stomped off, this time bowling over his friends, who were still pressed up behind him so close they were practically on his back.

"Thanks, Julie," Greg said, stumbling just a little from nervousness. "I didn't know you got pictures that day at the cemetery."

Julie laughed. "I didn't," she said. "I was bluffing."

·   ·   ·

Greg and I kept looking over our shoulders the rest of the day at school. When I went to my locker, he stood guard. When he went to his locker, I stood guard. It made us late to most of our classes, but at least Belman wasn't able to sneak up on us. He probably wouldn't have anyway, thanks to Julie.

The three of us met up again that afternoon at the Kitchen Sink. The excitement of the encounter with Belman had worn off and we were all pretty down again about John Wollman. It had been a few days since we last saw him. As we locked up our bikes outside Uncle Dex's store, I remembered the money Greg and I had made from busking and pulled it out of my backpack to give to Julie.

She actually teared up. "You guys did this to surprise me?" she said. "That's so sweet."

"It's not the whole fifty," I said. "Just thirty-seven dollars. But that's all we could make. But I bet we could make more if we went out again."

Julie brightened. "Can I come, too? We could do a lot of business all performing together. Plus, it would be great practice. Live rehearsal."

We agreed we'd give it another try soon, then headed inside the Kitchen Sink.

"Hey, kids," Uncle Dex said as we walked in, sounding more cheerful than usual, which is saying a lot since if being cheerful was an Olympic sport he'd take the gold medal. Maybe the silver. No way just the bronze.

Then he gestured toward the back of the store. "You have a visitor."

It was Reverend Simpson, tucked into a big, overstuffed chair that had been there for so long it probably had a foot of dust underneath. He was holding one of Uncle Dex's big clocks, though he didn't seem to be doing anything with it. Just holding it.

"Afternoon, kids," he said.

We said good afternoon back.

Reverend Simpson opened the back of the clock and slowly, carefully, wound it up so it started working again. He checked his watch for the time, then opened the face of the clock and reset the hands so they were correct. After that, he carefully placed the old clock back on the table beside him.

"I'd invite you all to sit down," Reverend Simpson said with a chuckle, "but there are so many of these antiques piled on the chairs, doesn't seem to be enough room."

"We don't mind standing," I said.

"Or we can just sit on this rug," Julie added quickly. I realized she was afraid Reverend Simpson might stand up with us out of politeness, and he probably needed to stay sitting.

We all sat on the rug.

"The reason I came," Reverend Simpson began, "is ever since you children visited with me the other day, something's been nagging at me, but I couldn't quite figure out what it was. Then, finally, after I prayed on it — because I knew it was something important — it came to me. Why, I actually sat up in bed and said out loud, 'Now I remember!' My poor wife, woke her out of a dead sleep. She thought I was going crazy."

"What was it?" Greg asked.

Reverend Simpson pulled an old clothbound notebook out of his coat pocket. "This old diary of mine I kept off and on — from back in the war."

He opened it slowly, going through the pages cautiously,

probably afraid of tearing the old, brittle paper, until he found what he was looking for.

"A name came to mind when you kids visited. It may have been mentioned: Mr. John Wollman. From the medical corps. Turns out we were once aquainted."

"John Wollman?" I asked, incredulous. "But how?"

"I met him in the war," Reverend Simpson said. "Very briefly. But I did meet him. According to what I wrote, it was in 1943 and it was in April of that year, near the end of the Tunisian campaign."

He adjusted his glasses and seemed to be reading for the next few minutes.

"They needed blood donations for transfusions," he continued, "but they'd already gotten as much as medically possible from white soldiers. And this young medic — it was Corporal John Wollman, a nice young man — came from the field hospital down to where they had us Negro troops quartered, about a half mile away. Don't recall exactly where they had us, but wasn't a terribly long ways from the fighting, up to the north in Tunisia. He asked our captain if any of the Negro troops — that's what they called us, you remember — would be willing to donate. Well, of course, the captain voluntold each and every one of us, and so we lined up for hours one evening while Corporal Wollman drew blood to take back to the surgical unit. I remember speaking to him about where he was from and where I was from, and how he came to be in the medical corps. He told me he was one of those Pennsylvania Quakers, which I had never met before, and I was fascinated to hear about what all they believed and how they held their Friends meetings and such. Nothing like I'd ever known growing up in the South, of course."

"And then what?" Greg asked.

"And then he finished up with me and I went back to work," Reverend Simpson said.

"And that was it?" Julie asked.

Reverend Simpson shook his head. "Wish it had been, but no. That wasn't all. Turned out what they needed the blood for — or rather who they needed it for — was German prisoners they'd taken in the fighting. A whole lot of them by that time, with more pouring in all the time."

"I don't get it," I said. "I mean, was that a problem or something?"

"Against military regulations," Reverend Simpson said, still shaking his head.

"What was?" Greg and I both asked.

"Using Negro blood that way," he responded.

"You mean it was illegal to use blood from black soldiers for transfusions for white soldiers?" Julie asked, catching on a lot quicker than Greg or me. "Even if they were prisoners of war?"

"Hard to believe today, I know," Reverend Simpson said. "But that was the law. Scientists back then all said that there wasn't any difference between Negro blood and white folks' blood, so no health reasons for keeping it separate. They said blood was just blood. All you need to know is the blood type, but not the race. They said the race didn't matter. But politicians, and a lot of folks back in America, and a lot of folks in the military, they were all worked up and worried about mixing the races, mixing up the blood like that. Even if it was for saving the lives of those German prisoners of war."

"What happened to John, I mean Corporal Wollman?" Julie asked.

"Well, we heard about that, too — that while there were plenty in the medical corps who would look the other way about a thing like that because it was helping folks, there was a colonel they had over there who found out they'd used 'black blood' for white German soldiers and he was hopping mad about it. He had that poor young man arrested. Said Corporal Wollman collected blood from the Negro troops without permission from his commanding officer. Said they were going to court-martial him. Give him a dishonorable discharge from the medical corps and out of the army. Send him home in disgrace."

"But there wasn't anything disgraceful about what he did!" Greg exclaimed. "He was trying to save lives!"

Reverend Simpson had about as sad a look on his face as I'd ever seen. He reached out and patted Greg on the shoulder. "I know he was, son. We all knew he was. And you'd think we'd be able to put aside those sorts of prejudices when we're having to fight a war. But people being people, some are always going to bring the prejudices along with them no matter what they're doing and no matter where they go."

"Do you know what happened to Corporal Wollman after that?" I asked.

"Unfortunately, I can't help you there," Reverend Simpson said. "Right on the heels of that happening was the last big fight of the war there in Tunisia. We had the Germans and the Italians pushed all the way back almost to

Bizerte and Tunis, and everybody's attention was on finishing the job."

Uncle Dex had finished with his customer, and he came over and interrupted us. It was obvious that Reverend Simpson had tired himself out. His head was starting to droop again, and his hands had gotten shaky. "I'm going to drive Reverend Simpson back to the church," Uncle Dex said. "I think we need to let him catch a little break from the interrogation."

We all nodded and said, "Thank you." Greg added, "We really appreciate you taking the time to talk to us. We know how hard this must be." He looked a little sad when he said it and I think it's because he was thinking of his dad.

He helped Reverend Simpson stand, and we followed them to the door. Reverend Simpson turned to us just before they left.

"When you see John Wollman again, please give him my best regards," he said. "I'll be praying that he has found his peace. You can tell him that, too, if you wouldn't mind."

CHAPTER 22

We were all quiet for a moment when the door swung shut behind Uncle Dex and Reverend Simpson. Then we exploded.

"How could they do something like that?" I said once I could get over being so totally outraged that I could speak.

"That's about the most racist thing I've ever heard of," Greg said.

"There is something so wrong with people," Julie said, her voice softer than ours. Greg and I were nearly shouting, we were so mad.

"I guess not everybody was that way," I said, trying to calm down some and look at the situation fairly.

But Greg wasn't having any of it. "Some people might have thought differently, but, Anderson, come on. It was the government policy. It was military law. You heard what Reverend Simpson said. It wasn't just one guy being a jerk."

"A racist jerk," Julie added.

"Yeah, a racist jerk," Greg said. Then he launched into a string of other adjectives, like "stupid," "moronic," "twisted," "bigoted," and a whole lot of other words that I was familiar with but couldn't repeat.

"Better take it easy there, son," a voice behind us said. "That's some strong language you're using."

We all jumped up and down when we heard him. "John!" Julie exclaimed. "You're back!"

We wanted to hug him, of course, but as soon as we got close we all stopped, realizing it couldn't happen. It was an awkward moment until Greg said, "Pretend group hug!" and opened his arms and did exactly that — hugged the air, and us — near where John was standing. Julie and I did it, too.

"Good to see you kids again," John said. "I have missed you all."

"Where have you been?" Julie asked.

John shook his head. "Close by, mostly. But it's just been too hard to bring myself all the way here. Don't know if that makes sense, and I can't exactly explain it. Or explain why I'm able to be here with you now."

"Well, we're just glad you showed up," Greg said. "I'm just sorry you had to hear us talking about Colonel Buncombe. I'm so mad about what he did."

"I guess he was just raised up that way," John said. "Many were."

"But he was the one who brought you up on charges, just because you got black soldiers to donate blood for German POWs!" Greg protested, not willing to let Colonel Buncombe off the hook for anything.

"I know, I know," John said. "And believe me, I was outraged about it as much as you kids at the time. It still gets me angry to think about it today." He paused for a second and then asked, "That's not the regulation anymore, is it? I mean, I sure hope not."

"No way!" Greg said. "I bet they changed that a long time ago."

"I'm sure they did," Julie said, glancing at her iPhone, but resisting the urge to look it up right then and there on the Internet. There was time for that later.

"Good to hear," John said. "I'd have hated to think . . ." He trailed off.

"So, um, since you must have heard what Reverend Simpson told us?" I began.

John nodded. "Most of it."

I continued, "Well, I was wondering if it helped you remember, you know, the rest."

John thought about it for a minute, then nodded some more.

"I do," he said. "But it's like, well, like in Corinthians: 'through a glass, darkly.' You all know that Bible verse?"

We all shook our heads, though Julie said she had heard the expression before and was pretty sure she knew what it meant.

"'For now we see through a glass, darkly,'" John said, quoting the passage.

"But you can remember at least some of what happened after Colonel Buncombe had you arrested?" Julie said.

"It's hazy still," John said. "And like flashes, or scenes, or minutes of what happened. Not too clear, in other words."

"Like through a glass darkly," Greg said. "Now I get it."

"I was confined to medical corps quarters near the field hospital in northern Tunisia, a couple of miles behind the front lines," John said. "Waiting on the military police to take me away. Only they didn't come — not that day, and not the next day. I remember writing that letter to my brother, Aaron, the one you read, or read part of, anyway. About the court-martial."

He paused, as if trying to remember what had been redacted. Whatever it was, it didn't come to him.

"Anyway, on the third day, I was going stir-crazy, and the MPs still hadn't come. So I just up and left. I could hear the sounds of the battle, and knew it was miles away, but that's the direction I headed. I had my medic's kit with me — I always carried it no matter where I went, because you never knew when you'd need it. Troops passed me in trucks and tanks, hurrying to the front, and other troops passed me going the other way, many of them infantry, on foot, some dragging their weapons behind them. And there was ambulance after ambulance after ambulance, carrying wounded soldiers, or soldiers who had died."

He paused again, and this time it seemed as if he was actually looking right at the lines of survivors and ambulances streaming past him, his heart going out to every one of them.

"I heard it before I saw it," he began again. "A German Stuka, machine guns blazing, swooping in to strafe the road and everybody on it. I'd heard that sound a hundred times, maybe a thousand. I dove to the side of the road and covered my head. We all did, which probably didn't make any difference, probably didn't give us any more protection than if we'd just stood there, but it's just your instinct to duck away from something like that."

"Did anyone get hit?" I asked.

John nodded. "I ran across the road over to them. It was one of the ambulances, hit and on its side and burning. Me and a couple of others dove inside to pull out the guys in there — the driver and the medics and the wounded soldiers. We got most of them out, too, but there was one more still inside."

John stopped there. He couldn't seem to say anything else.

"You went back for him, didn't you?" Julie asked gently.

He nodded.

"Did the plane come back, too?" Greg asked. "The Stuka?"

"Yes," John whispered.

"Nobody knew it was you in there, did they?" I asked.

He shook his head, and then regained his voice, though he was still whispering as he finished his story. "They always flew in formation," he said. "But this one was a lone wolf.

We must have destroyed most of their planes by then, but this one somehow slipped through. He must have gotten hit when he circled back around for another pass, because I heard the screaming sound of him diving, free-falling, straight at the ambulance."

"And that was the last thing?" Julie asked.

"Yes," John whispered. "That was the last thing. I was still inside with the last man. And like you said, nobody knew I was there."

We were all crying by now, and once again, it was too hard to speak. So we didn't. The four of us sat in silence for a really long time, as the shadows grew longer inside the Kitchen Sink. I wondered how it must feel to John, if sitting there like that with us reminded him of those long ago Friends meetings when he was a boy growing up in Philadelphia in his Quaker family with his mom and his dad and his brother. I remembered what we were supposed to tell John — what Reverend Simpson had asked us to pass on to him about finding peace.

I turned to tell him that, but too late. John Wollman was gone, and I had a feeling this time it was for good.

CHAPTER 23

Julie sent the money for the letters to John Wollman III, and included a letter of her own to tell him what we'd found out, even though Greg and I both told her not to bother.

"I just think John would have wanted us to," she said. "And you never know what might come of it. Somebody in his family should know what a hero John was, even if we don't have the kind of proof we'd need to go to the army and have his record changed or whatever."

We went with her to the post office to drop off the letter, then we all went home to get ready for the open mic competition that night. We only had two songs to perform — Julie still hadn't taught us the rap song that she was supposed to be working on — but surprisingly none of us seemed stressed out about it. In fact, the subject never even came up during rehearsal for some reason.

I wondered for a long time about what Reverend Simpson said to us — about giving his regards to John the next time we saw him. How could Reverend Simpson know we would see John Wollman, or had ever seen him? Plus, I wasn't sure we'd even mentioned John's name to Reverend Simpson in the first place.

In the end, though, I decided to just let that mystery be.

. . .

We were one of the last to play that night at the open mic competition and had to wait a really long time because there were more bands than when we'd played before — eight of them. Belman's band, the Bass Rats, played right before us, and I hated to admit it but once again they were pretty clearly the best band there.

"What I wouldn't give for a carton of eggs and another rubber chicken," Greg muttered to me halfway through their set. That got me laughing so hard that when it was our turn to perform I forgot to be nervous, and managed to make it through our two songs as lead singer without throwing up.

Then, without us even discussing it, we all just started playing "Simple Gifts" — softly and slowly at first, and then Julie started picking up the tempo a little, and then picking it up a lot until it turned into a different song almost. Then, moved by the spirit or whatever, she, all of a sudden, jumped up from her keyboard and grabbed the mic and the mic stand, and the next thing I knew she was rapping. So that was her rap song! I nearly fell over when I realized what was going on.

"It's the gift to be simple, it's the gift to be free, it's a gift to come down where we ought to be."

I doubted the Quakers had ever heard anything like it at any Friends meetings, but the open mic competition crowd seemed to like it okay.

We came in third.

AUTHOR'S NOTE

The war in North Africa was a huge part of World War II, and the beginning of the United States' involvement in the fight to take back Europe from the Germans, although it's not as widely studied in schools or the focus of as many books and movies as other areas of the war. However, it's still incredibly important in the bigger picture of World War II, and the efforts of the men and women who served — and sacrificed — in North Africa should be recognized.

The war in North Africa between the Allies and the Axis powers began on June 10, 1940, though the United States didn't send troops into battle there until November 1941.

Many of the Allied countries had colonies in North Africa, so in addition to being a route to get troops to Italy, they were also looking to protect their colonies. The fighting took place primarily in the northern part of Africa, although *AWOL in North Africa* revolves mainly around events in Morocco, Algeria, and Tunisia. The North Africa campaign ended with an Allied victory over the Germans and Italians on May 13, 1943.

As with other Ghosts of War books, much of this story is fiction, including the present-day characters, the mystery, and the ghost. However, the historical figures and major events in the book are all based on fact. There are many excellent books about the war in Northern Africa and the Tunisian campaign, and about those who fought there: George Patton, Dwight D. Eisenhower, Erwin Rommel, Bernard Montgomery, and, of course, the many brave soldiers and officers on the ground. Rick Atkinson's authoritative work *An Army at Dawn: The War in North Africa, 1942–1943*, winner of the Pulitzer Prize for nonfiction, was an invaluable resource. It's a worthy read for any readers who want to learn more about the early years of America's involvement in World War II.

For a sneak peek of the next

GHOSTS of WAR

adventure, turn the page . . .

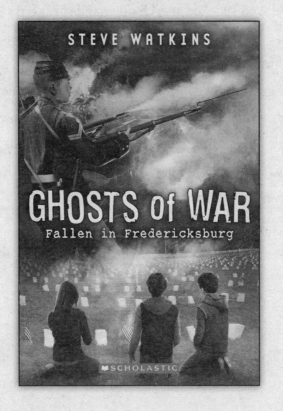

Julie, who is one of the most
serious people I know, had been working on being not quite
so serious, and when we got back down to the basement she
told us a joke.

"I bet you guys don't know why ghosts make bad liars."

Greg and I looked at each other and shrugged.

Julie got this big grin on her face. "Because you can see
right through them!"

We groaned, of course. Somebody else made a noise, too.

We whirled around to see a man — or more like a
teenager — in a dirty blue Union army uniform, his tattered
hat cocked to one side like it had been knocked over there
and never straightened.

"Where is my little brother?" he demanded.

We were so caught off guard that nobody could speak
right away, not even Julie.

The ghost was standing over the old trunk, as if looking
for something. The lid was open and there was a strange
golden light inside. He took a step toward us — a menacing
step, or that's how it seemed — and said it, or demanded it,
again.

"Where is my little brother?"

We were all still scared speechless, trying to think of something, anything, to say back.

The ghost stood firm and waited, hands on the hips of his dirty pants, which seemed a couple of sizes too big. The uniform coat seemed too big, too. For some reason there was a sprig of wilted green leaves tucked into the collar. The ghost was short and it was obvious that he didn't shave or didn't need to — that's how young he was. But he still looked like he wanted to fight somebody. I wanted to assure him that we weren't part of the Confederate army. I mean, I was from the South, sure, but I wasn't a Rebel or anything. I didn't even like the Rebels, or what they stood for and what they fought for.

But it didn't seem like the time or place to tell the Union soldier — or ghost — all that.

Julie finally found her voice. "We don't know where your little brother is," she said calmly — way calmer than Greg or I could have been, or were likely to be for another hour. "And we don't know who he is. But maybe we can help you figure it out."

"Help me?" the ghost said, his voice so high that I thought he could almost pass for a girl.

"Yes, help you," Julie said. "We've helped some other ghosts. They had things in that trunk." She pointed and the ghost turned to look at the trunk, which was still open, and still giving off that golden light.

Julie continued, "Is there something of yours in there?"

The ghost continued staring for a minute, and then nodded. "I lost it in the battle, but there it is." He thought for a minute, then added, "I can't pick it up."

"Can you tell us what it is?" Julie asked.

"They told us to fix bayonets," the ghost said. "That's all I remember."

I knew all about bayonets, which are like long knives, or more like the end of a spear, and you attach it to the end of your gun so you can use it as a weapon for close fighting. "Fix bayonets" is the order they give when soldiers are supposed to get out their bayonets and put them on their rifles.

"Is there a bayonet in the trunk?" Julie asked. "Is that what you're missing?"

"It wouldn't have mattered if I'd had it," the ghost said, not answering Julie's question. "Nobody got close enough. Nobody at all."

And with that the ghost vanished, the golden light blinked out, the trunk lid slammed shut on its own.